THE CHRISTMAS JUKEBOX

THE CHRISTMAS JUKEBOX

JASON F WRIGHT
JOHN S WRIGHT

Copyright © 2020 by Jason F Wright

All rights reserved.

No part of this book may be reproduced in any form or by any electronic or mechanical means, including information storage and retrieval systems, without written permission from the author, except for the use of brief quotations in a book review.

ISBN-13: 979-8-5721-8005-3

To Mom. It all started with you.

CHAPTER 1

Mackenzie, "Mac," Talley pulled a manila folder from the middle of a cardboard box and settled into her antique office chair. It rumbled along the uneven plank floor and groaned as she leaned back to put her feet on the desk. "Let's see what we have here." Mac usually only talked to herself when she was on the road, but lately found herself doing it more often and in more places. She looked across the top of the folder at the rough wooden pillar that Richard would lean against, arms folded across his narrow chest, covering whatever was printed on that day's tee shirt.

Tears began to form in her eyes, but a tightening of her jaw and a "Nope" said to the empty room stopped them. She would probably cry sometime today, but not now. Not over a shadow and a box full of shuffled business records.

"Hey, Nicole, are you out there?"

"Yes, Ma'am," Nicole replied without looking away from her computer.

"Can you come and help me wade through some of this… stuff?"

As she walked the few feet from her desk - which was actually an antique door attached to antique sawhorses - to Mac's, she wondered why Mac had changed her mind. She had insisted just a few hours earlier that she didn't want or need any help. Nicole had, in fact, offered to go through and catalog all the papers that Richard left behind.

"Worse than you thought?"

Mac held up a folder stuffed with papers. "This one folder has old bills, new bills, old receipts, old *recipes* - I guess because recipe sounds like receipt - and about a million business cards. Some look really old, but I recognized some as current and useful. I'm guessing he never asked you to put them in the computer."

"Good guess. Where do you want me to start?"

"I don't know. It's just more overwhelming than I thought it would be." She stretched out the word 'overwhelming' and Nicole thought she heard an emotional crack in the middle.

"How about this," Nicole said. "Let's just go through everything and make three piles. Stuff we can pitch right away... like that takeout menu, stuff we should deal with right away, and stuff we can ignore for a while."

Mac lit up as if Nicole had just discovered a cure for cancer. "Awesome. You are awesome. Thank you so much." Nicole blushed at the first genuinely kind words from Mac in weeks.

"Saw it on Pinterest." She grinned.

They started with the folder Mac had been struggling with and three piles began to form as they settled into a comfortable rhythm.

"Trash?"

"Trash."

"Keep?"

"No, trash."

"What about this one?" Nicole held up an invoice from the shop they used to refinish the most valuable antique furniture they bought.

"Let me see that. It must be old because we haven't sent them anything in months." She looked it over and asked, "Did we pay this? It says it's the second notice for work done in May." It was now November.

"Hold on." Nicole took the invoice to her computer and, after a minute, shouted, "Not paid. In fact, we haven't cut them a check all year."

"That might explain why Richard asked me to find another refinisher," Mac said as she shrank deeper into her chair. "I wonder what other wonderful surprises my ex-wonderful ex-partner left for us."

"He was full of them when he was here, so we can probably expect plenty now that he's bolted." Nicole was glad for the chance to vent some of her own feelings about the man who had been her boss and, she believed, her friend.

Mac didn't pile on, though. She just set her jaw, put the invoice in the "right away" pile, and plucked a few more sheets from the folder. She said, "I hope there aren't many more surprises like that one."

There were.

"How bad does it look?" Mac was in a hopeful mood after walking through the warehouse. She would have to hustle, but the gallery had a lot of inventory on hand. It was also a good time to buy more, assuming she could come up with some cash. In November, people were looking to sell their unused items to make a little Christmas money. In December, other folks would come into the showroom looking for that perfect gift for the friend who has everything. It wasn't the very best time of year to be a picker, but Mac and Richard usually made enough to survive the winter and be ready to scoop up the great finds that appear in the spring.

The look on Nicole's face erased half of Mac's optimism. Her words wiped out the rest. "The good news is that we ought to be able to collect a few thousand dollars from thrift stores and auction houses that haven't paid us yet."

"And the bad news?"

"It will barely make a dent in what we owe other people."

"I don't understand. It's not like I've been living under a rock. Money comes in and money goes out. Richard never said a word about getting behind."

3

Nicole swept an arm over the piles of paper on the table. "Well, it didn't look terrible until I got to August. That's when I started finding invoices that hadn't even been taken from their envelopes." She pulled one from the stack and handed it to Mac. "Remember when I had to take a few weeks off to help with my grandma? Richard started picking up the mail and said you two would take care of everything for a while."

"I remember. He insisted that I keep buying while he ran the shop."

"The bottom line is that the bills you or I opened got paid. The ones he saw first ended up in the bottom of that drawer."

"How many?"

"A couple dozen."

"How much?"

Nicole squinted at a Post-It note. "Twenty-eight thousand." She met Mac's worried gaze. "Give or take."

Mac sunk into her chair and stared at the envelope in her hand. She ran her thumb along the smooth plastic window in the middle. Sloan Antiques c/o Richard Polson and Mackenzie Talley.

"There's some sort of code on the back of the ones he buried," Nicole said.

Mac turned the envelope over. A white-hot rage pushed away fear and self-pity. "MP," she growled.

"Yeah, MP. What does it mean?"

"It was something Richard said when he wanted to end a conversation and move on. 'Mac's Problem.'"

Nicole regarded the papers that Mac had swept off the desk during her storm of righteous anger. As she picked them up, something felt off about the way Richard skimmed money from what was as much his business as Mac's. She put all of the unpaid bills in one pile and tried to see if they had anything in common. Nothing jumped out at her. Some were large and others small. It appeared almost random, as if Richard had held two envelopes in his hand and said, "Eenie, meenie, minie, moe," and then paid one while stashing the other in the bottom of a drawer.

Her opinion of Richard hit bottom when he left but she had a hard time imagining him smiling at Mac one day and then destroying her life and livelihood the next. Would he up and leave for greener pastures? Obviously. Would he leave destruction in his wake? Nicole was less sure about that.

An idea came to her and she looked at the door to Mac's office. She may or may not have a problem with what Nicole was about to do, but this was one of those situations where forgiveness later was better than permission now. She took one of the unpaid invoices off the stack and dialed the number printed under the logo made up of two wood chisels crossed like swords. "Yes, hello. This is Nicole from Sloan Antiques. I'm calling about an invoice you sent us for..." She tugged it out of the envelope, cursing herself for not being better prepared. "...some repairs you made to a dining table in August."

A long pause was followed by "Hold on a sec." Nicole smiled as the small-shop version of music-on-hold leaked through the hand over the receiver. The guy who answered the phone was shouting at someone else to get Tyler. While Tyler was being located and sent to a phone, Nicole got to listen to the muffled sound of some piece of woodworking equipment humming in energetic spurts. Then, still muffled, the man Nicole assumed was Tyler said, "Why do you still do that? These phones all have hold buttons."

"I know, Boss, but I usually cut people off if I push any buttons."

Tyler came on the line with a sigh. "This is Tyler. Is this Richard?"

"No, this is Nicole. I work for Mac and Richard." This was going to be more awkward than she had hoped.

"Oh. Is Richard okay?"

"I don't know. He... um... moved on."

"He's dead?!"

"No, no. I'm so sorry. He left unexpectedly. Mac and I are trying to discover any loose ends he may have left."

"He left? Where did he go?"

"We don't know. I'm sorry. I had kind of hoped you might be able to shed some light on the situation."

"No. The last time we talked, he told me the business had a temporary cash flow problem and asked if he could have a couple of months to settle up. We go way back so I said, 'sure, no problem.'"

"I see. Well, as I said, we're still going over the books to see where we stand. It might be a few more days before we can talk about what we owe you. I hope that's alright."

"It has to be, I guess. You know, the last thing he said to me sounded weird, but now it makes some sense."

"What was that?"

"He smiled real big... you know how he does... shook my hand and said, 'Don't worry, Tyler. Mac can fix anything. She'll make this right.' I hardly ever talk to Mac because me and Richard are friends. It was funny that he didn't say he would make it right." He paused for so long that Nicole wondered if he was about to hang up. Then he asked, "Mac will make it right, right?"

"I'm sure she will. I'll ask her to call you as soon as we know which end is up, okay?" Nicole waited to make sure Tyler didn't have anything more than "Okay" and "Goodbye" to say and then hung up the phone. She looked at the other unpaid bills and noticed a pattern. A couple were from national suppliers that, she assumed, would just cut them off if they failed to pay. The other companies were all small local shops. She knew that Richard was friends with most of the owners and now guessed that he was close enough to all of them to sweet talk them into cutting him some slack.

"Why didn't he just clean out the bank account?" She wondered out loud. She launched the accounting software that Richard had insisted she use to manage the books. It had more features than she could ever learn or wanted to use but she certainly knew how to make it show transactions by date. She discovered cash withdrawals matching every unpaid invoice. She rushed over to Mac's office and thumped on the door, forgetting the dark cloud that was probably hanging over her boss.

"What?" Mac sounded more sad than angry.

"I think I figured it out," she said as she opened the door and spread papers out on Mac's desk.

"Figured what out?"

"What Richard was doing. I can't for the life of me imagine what he was thinking but, for whatever reason, he wanted to leave behind as little trouble as possible." She put a hand on the invoices. "He knew all of these owners personally and, I'm sure, promised them you would pay them in full if they would just give Richard a little more time."

"Wait, what? You think he told them *I* would pay them?"

"I know he told at least one of them that." She pulled Tyler's furniture repair bill from the stack. "I talked to this guy and he used almost exactly those words." Nicole held up a finger as Mac's jaw began to move. "Every time he wrote 'MP' on an envelope and stuck it in that drawer, he withdrew precisely that amount of cash from the bank. No more, no less."

"I still don't get it. Why make it so complicated? Why not just clean us out on his way out of town?"

"Exactly!" Nicole straightened her back in triumph.

"Exactly what?"

"I think taking money a little at a time and softening the blow with vendors was Richard's way of softening the blow for you."

"If he were here, I would tell him that knowing that he schemed for months does not 'soften the blow'."

"I looked at all the accounts and lines of credit. Yes, you owe a lot of people a lot of money, but I think you'll be okay. From what I heard when I first got here, you two flirted with failure a couple of times early on."

"Let's see if I have this straight. My partner, in business and life, pretended everything was great in both business and life. He bought and sold and smiled and kissed and talked about the future. All while he was pulling what I'm sure he thought was his fair share out of the business so he could walk out on me. But, the good news is that I should be able to keep the business we built together afloat, probably just so I will have to think of the loser every day. Please, keep the good news coming, Nicole."

The women's eyes stayed locked on each other. Mac's were cold, tired, and still streaked with red. Nicole's were clear, wide with surprise, and filling with unwanted tears. She said, "If you don't start looking past the first thing you see, you'll never get the whole picture." She slapped the desk. "You, of all people, should know that it's usually worth lifting up the tarp and cleaning off the dust to discover what's really there." Her hand slid gently across the smooth surface of the banker's desk Mac had rescued from a barn in Oklahoma. Then she turned and walked away.

CHAPTER 2

The Army-surplus duffle bag sat alone on the beat-up, mostly-white floor of the extended cargo van. As Mac closed the double rear doors, she tried to conjure up the feelings of excitement and anticipation that the empty van usually gave her. In a few days, she would park in the same spot and unload some combination of trash and treasure. The treasure would pay the bills right away and the trash would, hopefully, become somebody's treasure after Richard did some magic. He called it "picker's alchemy."

But to Mac, it was all about the hunt, the Big Find. The butterflies in her stomach that threatened to break her poker face into a grin as she got ready to negotiate. She was a good negotiator, honest but ruthless. Only once had she pretended that a rare antique was a common cedar chest. It was her first Big Find, and she expected Richard to congratulate her on becoming a real picker. The look of disappointment on his face crushed her. He said, "It's subtle but there is a difference between hoping something is worth way more than you're paying and knowing that you're cheating someone who doesn't know better." They sent half of the profit from that piece back to the seller. Mac had learned her lesson.

As she waved goodbye to Nicole through the window, she

wondered if the way Richard had abandoned her was his way of walking the line between hope and deception. Was he sitting in a bar somewhere telling himself he had forced a fair deal on his old girlfriend?

Nicole tapped on the driver's window. "Is something wrong with the van? You've been just sitting there for a while."

"No, everything's fine. Just deciding which way to go. Which way should I go, Nicole?"

"It's easiest to get out of town heading east."

"I'm in no hurry so west it is. Thanks. See you in a few days." She turned into traffic and made her way to the interstate. Mac never enjoyed this part of the trip. Sloan, Texas, was an island of quiet suburban streets in a sea of six lane asphalt. Maneuvering the big van through heavy traffic made her anxious almost to the point of nausea. And then she would hit clear, straight, Texas highway.

As soon as she merged onto a long, straight stretch of highway, her breathing slowed, and her hand punched the power button on the satellite radio. Mac rarely changed channels. The road called for a certain kind of music. Taylor Swift was halfway through a favorite song when Mac's face relaxed into the first completely natural smile she'd had in weeks.

She didn't know where she was going, what she was looking for, or how long she would search for it. She knew she had to bring back some things to sell, but that wasn't the main reason for the trip. By the time she got back, the most valuable thing in the van would take up no space at all. A decision.

Mac looked at the empty seat next to her. She imagined Richard sitting there, his head nodding out of sync with the music blasting out of the van's stereo. His noise-cancelling headphones were last year's Christmas gift from Mac. Actually, Mac now realized, the real gift was her unspoken permission for Richard to be physically with her in the van but to maintain his own world and music. The rumble of tires wandering toward the shoulder caused Mac to break eye contact with her memory. When she glanced over again, her backpack had replaced Richard on the seat and the loss she had half felt and half manufactured gave way to a tired melancholy.

She didn't know what she was supposed to be feeling. People had come in and out of her life before, but nobody she had loved as much as Richard had ever left her without warning. Even her most intense, three-pints-of-ice cream breakups had been processes more than events. Losing Richard was like being struck by lightning on a sunny day.

What had she done wrong? What signs had she not seen or unconsciously ignored? Why did he feel like disappearing was the best way to end the relationship? And how in the world was he able to smile at her from across from the office on Friday, cook dinner for her on Saturday, and vanish on Sunday? She had tried to get answers directly, but Richard left the company cell phone on his desk and emails to him came back with the cyberspace equivalent of "return to sender."

Mac decided not to wait until the warning light came on before getting gas. She got off the Interstate and was about to pull into a truck stop when she noticed a hand-painted sign on a tilting post next to the stop sign at the end of the ramp. "Gas, Food, Antiques." Exactly the combination Mac was looking for. She followed the winding two-lane road through the Oklahoma scrub and into one of the few small towns within a hundred miles of home that she had never visited.

She pulled up to a pump, popped the gas cap cover, and reached for the nozzle only to see a sign that said, "Sorry, no gas." *Good thing I didn't wait until I was running on fumes.* She looked around for someplace to park while she went inside, but decided the van was fine where it was since it wasn't in anybody's way.

The subtle scents of fall mixed with delicious smells coming from the diner pretending to be a restaurant. Mac took in a deep breath, happy to smell something other than gasoline and diesel fuel. From the outside, the large building seemed to be divided into roughly three equal sections: gas station, restaurant, and antique shop. As she pushed open the worn wooden door, though, she was disappointed to see that the "antique" section was the smallest area. It began near the gas station cash register, where some local handmade knickknacks shared shelf space with tourist-trap items made in China. In the next row were some actual antiques, but they were over-priced and of no interest to Mac. It took her all of two minutes to decide she had wasted an hour and a gallon of gas.

The food smelled good, though, so she made her way back through the building to the restaurant. Over a pretty good plate of mac and cheese, she decided that the ESSO sign on the wall across from her was the only "antique" in the place worth more than $100.

She drove back to the truck stop, filled the tank, stocked up on soda and chips, and munched while staring out the windshield at the traffic rushing back and forth across the overpass. After most of a day, she seemed further away from solutions and answers than ever.

What am I doing?

RATHER THAN GET BACK on the Interstate, Mac crossed under the overpass and continued in the other direction on the same state road that led her to the disappointing antique store. The map application on her phone showed an antiques mall in a town fifty miles away. She'd been doing this long enough to know that "mall" was a flexible term covering everything from a garage to a few outbuildings on the same property. The map entry showed no pictures or website but that wasn't unusual and, in fact, was a good sign because it likely meant that the owners were older and less likely to use eBay to price everything.

Carl's Antique Mall turned out to be a big 1920s era house at the end of a long gravel driveway. Mac slid the van in between two dusty cars that seemed to have found a comfortable place to rest and weren't interested in going anywhere else. As she put on her jacket and stretched the road out of her muscles, a pudgy man who looked to be in his 70s came out the back door of the house and ambled toward her.

"Afternoon. Are you Carl?"

"Ain't no Carl. Never was," he said as if for the millionth time.

"Oh. Where did the name…"

The man not named Carl cut her off. "My wife, rest her soul, was named Carla. Place used to be Carla's Antique Mall but the second 'A' wored off the sign so we just started calling it Carl's." Mac began to speak, but Not-Carl wasn't finished. "I asked Stubblefield down the road to make a new sign with both A's, you know, as a memory, but he just copied the old one. I figured it was supposed to be that way."

"I'm sorry for your loss. How long were you together?"

"Fifty-two years exactly." He looked at the ground and then, with a subtle shake of his head, back at Mac. "You looking for antiques?"

"Yes, sir, but I buy so I can sell them at my shop in Sloan or on the Internet."

"The Internet," he scoffed. "Ain't nothing good on the Internet. Stubblefield keeps telling me I could make more money, but I seen what it does to kids. Internet and cell phones. Got no use for any of it."

"I sometimes feel the same way, Mister…"

"Vic. Just Vic."

"… Vic. So, I'm looking for items you're willing to take cash for today even if you won't get as much for it as if you wait for just the right customer to come through the door."

Vic turned toward the house and said, over his shoulder, "Come look around if you want but I'm real patient. Won't sell for less than I would haggle with a tourist, even if it's a year before I see another one."

Mac followed Vic into the back of the house, easing the screen door closed behind her so it didn't bang against its frame. They walked through a small kitchen and into a long hallway with arched doorways on either side. Mac smiled as she inhaled the smell of intimate history. Dried flowers and Carla's perfume. Furniture wax and old fabric. "A lot of history here, Vic. How much of it is yours? I mean things you didn't buy just to sell again?"

"About half and half. Not including Carla's things." He gestured toward an archway with a sheet covering its opening. "Don't know if I'll ever sell any of that, even the stuff she didn't much care for."

Mac nodded but had shifted into a flow that Richard called magical. Her eyes scanned each room from top to bottom, left to right. "Where did you get this? What do you want for that? What's in that box up there?" In fifteen minutes, Mac had recorded a mental inventory of everything worth anything in Carl's Antique Mall. They haggled over a 19th century chair, but Carl was convinced it was worth more than Mac knew she could get for it. "Well, Vic, you know your stuff. Thank you for showing me around. You have some wonderful things here."

"Sure you don't want the bank? You don't see many of these things that still work." He picked up a mechanical Uncle Sam and turned a key in his back. Then, with the flick of small tin lever, Sam took off his hat and rested it on a crate. Vic put a dime in the hat's slot and it thunked and clinked as it joined at least one other coin in the bank's base. A familiar thrill threatened to turn the disinterested look on Mac's face into a broad smile. *Gotcha.*

"I don't know. It's in pretty good shape but, honestly, they aren't all that rare and the market is kind of weak right now." *All technically true.*

"Well, I hate for you to leave empty-handed. What if I come down to $150?"

"Tempting, but I don't think I would get much more for it than that." *Also technically true.* "How about $100?"

"$125."

"$120."

Vic grinned. "$122.50. Final offer. I don't want to do no more math."

"You know what, Vic, you're right. Round numbers are easier." Mac pulled a roll of cash from her left back pocket. If she had bought something costing more than $200, she'd have reached in her right back pocket. Over $500 would have been her front right. Beyond that would have meant a walk to the van. She peeled off two fifties, a twenty, and a five. "$125. Just like you said." Mac quit trying to hide her joy and let a smile take over her face. She had already done more mental math in a few seconds than Vic had in the past year. $125 for the bank and $75 to the guy who doesn't charge enough to clean and touch up antique toys put her cost at $200. The right buyer would be happy to pay $500 for it, and she could get $400 on eBay with no effort at all.

Vic's eyes widened with surprise as if the extra $2.50 had been $250. "Thank you. Good doing business with you."

"You're welcome. Hey, Vic, do you know any other collectors in the area who might be willing to sell? I'm looking for all kinds of things and when I say collectors, I also mean people who just don't ever throw stuff away."

"I can think of a couple folks, but you don't want their junk. Tell you what, though, you should go to that Christmas diner in Green Vista. It's on down the road; the first town after you cross into Texas. Stan and Moira are retiring, closing the place down. It's decorated with some really nice things that are probably worth more than they know. There's more stuff in their barn, too."

"Perfect. That's exactly the sort of place I'm looking for."

"Food's really good, too. Say hello from Vic," he said as Mac got in the van and closed the door. As she started the engine, Vic motioned for her to roll down the window. "Make sure you check out the jukebox," he said with a wink.

CHAPTER 3

Mac had seen dozens of small-town restaurants like Stan's Diner and could have found it without Vic's directions. A gaggle of houses was followed by a "reduce speed ahead" sign which was right next to an elaborate "Welcome to Green Vista" sign that had other signs and badges hanging from it like jewelry. The diner, Mac knew, would be one of the next three or four businesses. Every town seemed to need some combination of car repair, laundromat, Family Dollar, clothing boutique (Mac could never figure that one out), and a restaurant owned and managed by a local. Stan's broke the mold, but not by much. It was last in line and half a mile past the laundromat, just before the speed limit went back up. As she pulled into the parking lot, Mac could imagine the local cop waiting there to ticket people from both directions as they either sped up early or slowed down late.

The lot was empty except for an old Cadillac right next to the diner's double doors. She'd learned from sad experience to keep the van away from poles, so she parked it right between the tall sign and the Caddy. The sign had space under "Stan's Diner" for a few lines of changeable characters. Rather than a menu item or business hours, the words "Merry Christmas" in double-high letters filled the space.

The greeting was only slightly premature, but the sign looked like it hadn't been changed in months. Or ever.

Before going in, Mac peeked around the side of the building and down a short paved driveway. Anything bigger than a house was apparently a barn to Vic. A green steel building with hanger-style doors stood on the same concrete pad as the modest home a dozen feet away. Dim points of red and green lights were just becoming visible along the eaves as the shadows of a fall afternoon began to envelop the house. Reflexively, Mac looked down at her watch to make sure it wasn't a month later than she thought it was.

Opening the door to the diner triggered a tinny, electronic version of the first few notes of "Jingle Bells," not the chorus but the "Dashing through the snow..." part. The gray-haired woman behind the counter watched and waited patiently as Mac scanned the room. Where most people saw walls covered with Christmas spirit, if a little bit early and over the top, Mac saw individual items with imagined price tags hovering over them. When she got around to the jukebox in the corner, her mind overlaid a price tag with three dollar signs and an exclamation point.

"What can I get you, Hon? If you don't see what you want on the menu," she gestured with her head at the signs above and behind her, "let me know and I'll see how close I can come to making it for you."

Mac leaned forward so she could make out the woman's name tag. "Thank you, Moira - am I saying that right? - I'm sure it's all good. Just give me a second."

"It's not *all* good," a voice from behind her said. Mac turned around and noticed a man in a booth reading a newspaper. She had somehow looked right past him while taking inventory.

"Be nice," Moira said as she started the coffee grinder.

A pair of smiling eyes under bushy white eyebrows peeked over the paper. "Come on, Moira, admit that the tuna melt is hit or miss."

"Depends on who makes it."

"Ha. Ha." He put the paper down and turned his attention to Mac. "Skip the tuna melt and go for the burger. Make sure Moira or her lazy husband drop fresh fries for you, though. There's nothing worse than a perfect burger spoiled by soggy fries."

"Speaking of lazy husbands, how about you get back here and help make this young lady's visit her first of many."

Mac shifted out of the way as the man eased out of the booth. He tipped an imaginary hat as he said, "I'm Stan. How about that burger?" Stan unfolded to just over six feet tall, putting the top of Mac's head at chin level. "What do you want on that burger, Miss?"

"She may not want a burger, Stan."

"Everybody wants a burger, right?" He turned to Mac. "Even if you are a vegetarian, which is perfectly fine by me, we can fix you up with a delicious meat substitute on a toasted bun with my signature sauce."

"It's mustard and mayo mixed together," Moira chimed in.

"A burger would be great," Mac said, taking advantage of the first break in the couple's banter. "Lettuce, tomatoes, pickles, and extra Signature Sauce." She wasn't quite ready to eat again, but knew that gushing over a man's cooking was a great way to win him over.

"Comin' right up." Stan put on an apron and disappeared through a swinging door.

"That's quite the routine you've got there." Mac settled on a stool at the counter. "Do all your customers get the full treatment?"

"Dear, that was not the full treatment. He's got a lot more where that came from." Moira turned her head slightly and raised her voice a bit. "Just don't encourage him."

"I heard that!"

Moira's warm smile lingered as she locked eyes with Mac. "You're a first-timer. Just passing through?"

"Yes, Ma'am." Mac remembered why she was there and prepared to get down to business. "Actually, I'm looking for antiques and collectibles for my shop and studio." Confusion flickered across Moira's smile. Mac quickly added, "Vic from down the road told me you might be looking to… downsize."

"That's one way to put it," Stan said as he appeared from the back and put two patties on the grill. "Another way is to say we're closing up shop and hitting the road."

"Well, if closing up shop means you're willing to sell rather than store some of your collection, I would love the chance to have a look and make some offers."

The couple shared a serious look that seemed to Mac to replace a five-minute conversation. Stan said, "Let's chat after you finish this fantastic burger."

Stan did most of the chatting. He shared the story of how he started collecting things to decorate his diner for its grand opening 10 years ago. Then he bought more items to replace the ones he couldn't stand to look at anymore. Then he changed themes from '50s to Southern and Western.

Stan wrapped up the history lesson. "Once I found my Moira, we changed the theme to Christmas all year, but we didn't get rid of anything. The property came with a big storage building, so we didn't feel the need. Most of what's in there is most likely junk but we'll probably hire an auctioneer to come in and get what he can out of it."

"I'll tell you what," Mac said as she pushed her last fry through the last puddle of Signature Sauce. "Let me take a look at what you've got. I've been doing this for a long time and can tell you what's worth selling and what's not. If something looks like a good fit for my shop, I'll make you an offer. By the time we're done, you'll have a good idea of what your collection's worth. You might even have some extra money in your pocket."

Moira looked surprised when Stan answered. "Sounds like a plan. Moira, looks like we're closing up for a while. No way am I going to wander through your stuff without you."

As Stan adjusted the sign on the door so its clock hands told disappointed diners to come back at six, Mac hoped he or Moira didn't notice her staring at the jukebox. Or the jacket she left draped over a stool at the counter.

EVERYONE GOT something out of the visit to the barn. Mac picked up a few things she knew would sell for a nice profit. Stan got to show off his shrewd negotiating skills. Moira ended up with a few extra dollars and fewer things to go through when moving time came.

The Christmas lights shone bright now that the sun was over the horizon. The cool air, good company, and holiday spirit made Mac smile. The several hundred dollars of potential profit they were loading into the back of her van didn't hurt, either. As she closed the rear doors, she eyed an empty space just the right size for a jukebox and wondered if there was any chance this stop could get even better. "Here's the cash and receipt, Moira. Please look it over before I leave. It doesn't happen often but every once-in-a-while a miscount or misunderstanding causes problems we don't want to have." She paused while Moira counted. *Here we go!* "Oh, that's why I feel chilly. I left my jacket in the diner."

Without a word, Stan used a doorman gesture to direct the women toward the diner. He unlocked and opened it, holding it open while Moira went in and hit two light switches. The first turned on the harsh overhead fluorescent fixtures. The second filled the room with red, green, and white light from dozens of strings of Christmas lights hidden under ledges and behind furniture. A set followed the curved top of the jukebox, but it was otherwise a dark pocket surrounded by light.

Mac took her jacket from the stool and looked around the room as if for the first time. "Wow. It's amazing what a few strings of lights can do."

"Christmas is our thing. It's eccentric for nine or ten months of the year but around now our customers stop looking at us like we're nuts."

"So it's decorated like this all year?"

"Yep."

Mac turned toward the jukebox and was about to make her play when Stan said, "Time for pie."

"I really need to get back on the road…"

"After pie." If Stan had used that tone while haggling over the pony saddle a few minutes earlier, he might have gotten twenty more dollars for it.

"Sounds good." Mac settled back onto the stool. Moira lifted a glass cover and cut three pieces of apple pie.

"Ice cream?"

"No, thank you."

"I'd love some ice cream, Dear."

"I'm sure you would but you know our rule about dairy before bedtime."

Stan stuck out his bottom lip but didn't argue. Instead, he gave Mac a wink and whispered, "I'll sneak some later."

"Oh, and don't think you'll sneak any later," Moira said from the end of the counter.

Mac let the pie melt in her mouth as she wondered how aggressive she could be with this sweet couple that had already made her feel more comfortable than all but her closest friends. *We're all grownups. Let's get to it.* "What's the deal with the jukebox over there?" She bobbed her head in its direction but didn't look.

Stan looked at the machine almost lovingly. After a long moment, he answered, "I bought it not too very long before I found Moira. Since it has a Christmas theme, we sort of redecorated the rest of the place around it."

"Planning on taking it with you?"

"Hadn't really thought about it."

Here goes... "Willing to part with it? There's just enough room left for it in my van. It would keep me from having to strap the other stuff in. Sort of a space filler."

"A space filler, eh?" Stan's eyes glinted.

Mac knew she'd overplayed her hand but tried to recover. "Sorry it came out like that. Occupational hazard. It looks to be in pretty good shape, but jukeboxes don't sell for as much as you'd think. Collectors, it turns out, don't pay by the pound." She left out the fact that she had never seen or heard of a Christmas jukebox and couldn't even guess its manufacturer. It was bound to be rare. "How much would you take for it?"

Moira said, "It's not for sale."

Moira looked more confused than angry when Stan acted as if she hadn't spoken at all. He said, "How much will you give?"

"Does it work?"

Now, Stan looked at Moira and said, "Why don't you see for yourself. Moira, grab a quarter from the till. Mac, see if it's plugged in. Sometimes you have to unplug it and plug it back in."

Mac pulled the heavy cabinet away from the wall far enough to see the plug and outlet. The cord looked intact, if quite old, so Mac gingerly worked the plug out of the socket and then back in. With a thump, some clicks, and a whir, the jukebox came to life. Warm yellow-white light filled its center, illuminating a carousel of 45 rpm records. Behind the records was a Christmas scene that Mac hoped was hand-painted. Santa, a sleigh, and reindeer were suspended on a thin wire in front of a town full of snow-covered cottages. The top of the jukebox was arched like many others but instead of glowing tubes at the sides, shafts of green and red light shot from holes in the top of the arch.

"The lights dance with the music," Stan said as he walked over and handed Mac the quarter.

Mac found the coin slot but there appeared to be no other controls, just a mechanical display showing two faded zeroes. "How do you pick a song?"

"Near as we can tell, you don't. Just put a quarter in and out comes Christmas cheer."

Moira stood next to Stan and put her arm around his waist. "Go ahead, Dear, let's see if it will play a good song for you."

Mac pushed the quarter the rest of the way into the slot and listened to it rattle down the chute. Santa's sleigh moved along with the records as the carousel rotated until one tipped onto the platter. It had no label, but Mac knew the song before the first note made its way to the back of the diner. It was her favorite. White Christmas. She tried to push feelings and memories aside as the music played and the lights danced across the ceiling. She wanted to sit on the floor, watch the lights, and let the song wash over her. *Keep it together, Mac, it's just a song. The real star is this jukebox.* She stooped in front of the machine, poked at the coin return, and gently tapped on the glass. Just before the song ended, she said, "It's in pretty good shape and definitely unique. That's good and bad for me. I know how much I can get for a 1956 Wurlitzer, but I have no idea how much this is worth. Plus, I have to clean it up and then hope the right Christmas lover comes by. I can give you nine hundred bucks." *He'll counter with twelve and we'll settle at an even thousand. I know I can get a couple grand for it. Maybe more. Maybe a lot more.* Mac was so caught up in the game that she didn't notice the display change from zero-zero to one-two.

Stan put his arm around Moira so they were in a sort of side-by-side embrace. He shifted his gaze from the jukebox to Moira and said, without looking at Mac, "Deal."

CHAPTER 4

"I can't make it in early tomorrow, Mac. I'll be lucky to get there in time to open the gallery at ten. Plus, you said this was going to be a three- or four-day trip. I wasn't expecting you back so soon."

"That's okay, I guess. I'm just anxious to get this jukebox into the shop for a closer look. It could be a real winner."

"Just don't try to unload it yourself. We don't want a repeat of the Cherry Hutch Incident."

"You mean the one we don't ever talk about?"

"Yeah. That one. Hey, what about Aaron? He might be willing to help," Nicole suggested.

"I don't know. He's one of Richard's friends. I'm afraid it might be awkward for both of us."

"Richard ghosted you both, Mac. And I happen to know that Aaron misses the extra odd job cash."

"I'll think about it. See you tomorrow." By the time she finished the sentence, Mac had decided. She couldn't let Richard affect every decision from wherever he was. Aaron would bring not only the extra hands she needed, but he almost certainly knew a lot more about mechanical and electrical guts than she did. She rolled over and tried

THE CHRISTMAS JUKEBOX

to decipher the cheap motel clock on the cheap motel nightstand. All the segments of the first two digits were bright red. It was not 88:15, Mac decided, but, based on Nicole's crankiness, it could be fifteen after eleven, twelve, or even one in the morning. She was pretty sure it wasn't past midnight, but she was still groggy from her unanticipated nap.

She tried not to imagine the source of the carpet's crusty texture as she retrieved her phone from the table across the room. 11:15. Not too late.

"...Hullo?"

Maybe a *little* too late. "Aaron?"

"Uh, huh. Who's this?"

"It's Mac. Mackenzie. Richard's... former partner."

"Sure. What's up?"

She was about to apologize for the late call, but Aaron sounded wide awake now. "I just finished a buying run and have something I need help with. Are you available tomorrow morning?"

"Sure. I picked up a dinner shift at Bradberry's, but I can help until afternoon. What time should I be there?"

"I ran out of steam about three hours east of home but can get an early start. Plan on eight o'clock unless you hear otherwise."

"Good deal," Aaron said. "Thanks."

"I should be thanking you. So, thanks. See you tomorrow." She hung up the phone and turned on the TV, angry with herself for not being able to push through the last couple hundred miles. Lately, her relationship with sleep was like what she had with Richard. She needed it but could not control when it came, how long it stayed, or when it decided to leave.

AS SHE WATCHED Aaron amble up the sidewalk, Mac wondered if she might have been better off waiting for Nicole. He wasn't much taller than Mac and had nerd written all over him. He picked up his pace when he saw Mac and the van.

"Morning. Hope I didn't keep you waiting." He almost tripped over his own feet as he tried to check the time on his phone while speed-walking.

"I'm early. You're fine. Thanks again." She had already attached the ramp to the van and maneuvered the jukebox toward the center of the vehicle's floor.

"Cool." Aaron eyed the jukebox as he started to climb into the van.

"Why don't you stay down there and help guide the dolly. Let's just ease it down the ramp."

The jukebox rolled smoothly down the ramp, ending the trip with the slightest jolt. Aaron said, "That wasn't bad at all."

"I feel bad getting you up early. Looks like I could have managed it myself."

"No, you did right. If that thing got away from you, it would end up a pile of glass and kindling."

"Since you're here, do you mind helping me get the jukebox and everything else into the building?"

"Absolutely. I mean no, I don't mind. I will absolutely help you."

"Gotta earn those thirty bucks, right?"

"Thirty?" Aaron grinned. "I don't get out of bed for less than thirty-two-fifty. That is unless breakfast is involved."

"Thirty-two-fifty, it is." Mac grinned back.

When the van was empty and Mac's other purchases were stashed away, she and Aaron admired the jukebox. This was the only time of day when sunlight streamed directly in through the big garage door. Mac ran her hand up one side, along the top, and down the other side. The polished wood was smooth with the slightest film of what she assumed was years' worth of diner grease. "No deep scratches, cracked glass, or missing pieces," she said to herself even though Aaron was still there.

"I can't find any manufacturer markings or anything back here," he said from behind the machine. "There is a faded square just above the power cord. Maybe a label fell off."

"I'm going to have to open it up at some point, anyway. Hopefully there's a clue inside." She took two twenties from the pocket of her jeans and tried to hand them to Aaron.

"What, no breakfast?" His grin was not as bright as the first time he used the line.

"No, I'm just anxious to figure out what I've got here." Her gesture took in the jukebox and the storage room behind it. "Eat an extra pancake for me."

Mac needed another Diet Coke. The first two got her from the hotel to the shop but now she was fading fast. The hotel had been quiet and comfortable enough, but her eyes had flown open at 3:30 and she had known that staying in bed was a waste of time. She had spent the hours before heading home surfing the Internet looking for anything like the jukebox. The closest she could find was a custom unit based on an old Seeburg, but it looked nothing like the one from the diner. She wondered if someone had rebuilt a Wurlitzer. It did have the arched top, after all.

Now, as she looked at it up close, Mac wondered if someone might have built it from scratch. No part of it looked like it had been built in a factory. She plugged it into an extension cord that snaked across the concrete floor. With the same odd sounds it made in the diner, the jukebox lit up and waited for a quarter. Mac dragged up a recliner waiting for new upholstery so she could be comfortable during her examination. She dropped the quarter she'd stolen from Nicole's desk into the slot. Nothing happened. She called Nicole and left her a voice mail asking her to pick up a roll of quarters. Mac decided to lay back for a few minutes while waiting for Nicole. She popped out the footrest and updated her mental list of recliner renovations, adding a good WD-40 treatment. Soon, green and red lights flickered through eyelids that she didn't remember closing. She opened them and saw the same lights painting the beams of the ceiling as had been dancing around the diner. "White Christmas" began to echo around the workshop. Mac leaned forward and peered through the glass front, expecting to see Santa and his mechanical sleigh moving around the records. There was no Santa. There was no sleigh. There were no records. An animated Christmas scene completely filled the middle of the jukebox. A little girl was trying to hold a dress against her chest with one hand while a doll dangled from the other. She spun in a circle while both dress and doll fluttered. A man and woman stood nearby with a glowing Christmas tree behind them. Everyone was smiling. Happy. Mac remembered that Christmas morning. She was six.

Mac squeezed her eyes shut and shook her head. When she looked again, the colored lights were gone as were the little girl and her parents. "I've got to get more sleep," she said to the jukebox. Its only answer was a contented electrical hum followed by a click as the mechanical counter changed from twelve to eleven.

THE ONLY HARD evidence that the jukebox had done anything at all was the number eleven in the gas pump-like display. Mac wished she either had another quarter or the special round key to the machine's coin box. She considered walking the two blocks to a convenience store but then her eyes settled on Uncle Sam, the bank she'd bought from Vic at Carl's Antique Mall. She used what was left of her thumbnail to turn the latch holding the door closed at the bottom of the bank. A penny and a dime fell into her palm, and either a nickel or a quarter bounced off the side of her hand. It hit the floor and rolled under an antique dresser waiting to be refinished. "Seriously?" She got down on her hands and knees to peer under the dresser, hoping that the coin hadn't rolled any further. Her hand and forearm barely fit under the narrowest section of ornate trim. "If you're just a nickel after all this, I'm not going to be happy." She trapped the coin under her forefinger and carefully dragged it out. It was a quarter.

Mac stayed on her knees and swiveled toward the jukebox. She put the coin in the slot and settled back on her heels as the machine got ready to play another record. She hoped that, from this angle, she could read the label before it fell out of view below the edge of the window. The record had no label. The ones on either side of it in the carousel had no labels. She watched Santa fly as she waited to hear which Christmas song was going to play. It took her a few seconds to recognize "Winter Wonderland." The music came at her from the jukebox's chest at first, but soon the sound enveloped Mac from all directions. As before, the mechanical animation behind the glass was replaced by an ultra-realistic diorama of a child holding a Christmas gift. This time, it was a boy with a small guitar. He started to hold it as if to strum, but then hugged it to his chest. Mac read his lips as he turned toward the woman behind him. "Thank you, Mommy."

"Thank Santa," his mother's lips replied as she placed a hand on each of his shoulders. The boy and his mother stood in front of a tree that would have been at home in the lobby of the Ritz Carlton. They were both smiling, but the mother's smile was more complex than that of her innocent son. Mac recognized when someone was enjoying a rare moment of happiness. She did not recognize the woman or the boy.

The music stopped. The counter whirred and clicked as the right digit changed from a one to a zero.

CHAPTER 5

Mac stared at her ceiling, waiting and hoping for a few good hours of recharging sleep. The twilight between asleep and awake was now familiar territory. Mac was comfortable there, even though she often felt chased from one to the other. She knew the difference between reality and a vivid dream. She had been wide awake when her eyes saw and ears heard what came out of the jukebox. If it had been a dream, she would have moved through the phase when her brain alerted her that her actual senses had just been deceived by vivid imposters. Unless she was still dreaming, and she knew she wasn't, there had to be some other explanation.

She replayed both jukebox scenes in her mind. She had known the image from her childhood was not a dream, but wasn't ready to consider any other possibility. It would be so much simpler if she could just chalk the whole thing up to her sleep issues. Buried memories emerge in dreams all the time. Seeing her younger self at Christmastime would not be at all unusual. But it hadn't felt like a dream, even though she had been on the edge of sleep.

The second vision was different. Who was the boy? Why had she seen him and his mother? What was going on?

As she rolled onto her side and curled up a little, she decided to figure it all out in the morning. She took a deep, exhausted breath and thought, "Now *this* is what sleep feels like."

~

NICOLE MET Mac at the door, flipping the sign from CLOSED to OPEN after she passed through. "I thought you would pop in here yesterday. Did everything go okay at the workshop?" The gallery and workshop/warehouse were just far enough apart to make moving between them inconvenient.

"It went fine. I picked up a few good pieces. We should be able to turn them around pretty quick and start paying down that pesky line of credit."

"How about Aaron. Was he able to help? Tell me you didn't unload by yourself… again."

"He was great. No issues." Mac paused to let Nicole know she was about to change the subject. "Hey, could you poke around and see what you can find about Christmas-themed jukeboxes? It doesn't look like any of the usual manufacturers made any, but maybe somebody specialized in custom builds."

"So that's what you needed help with? A jukebox? A *Christmas* jukebox? Cool!"

"Yeah, cool. Looks to be from the fifties or sixties. Maybe even seventies, but no later than that."

"Any pictures?" The question caught Mac off guard. How did she not have a single picture of the jukebox yet? She always took pictures before and after buying anything except the most common of objects. And this one was far from common.

"Not yet. Tell you what, we'll close the gallery for an hour at lunch and go check it out together."

"I'll see what I can find out in the meantime."

Mac spent the morning cataloging her purchases and catching up on other paperwork that only she could do. Every task took twice as long as usual because her mind was elsewhere. She had narrowed the possible explanations of the visions down to four, three if she eliminated dreams. First, the jukebox could be part of an elaborate scheme using high-tech projectors and video. Second, something could be wrong with her physically, like a brain tumor or some other illness. Third, she might be losing her mind.

First things first.

She leafed through the receipts and other bits of papers from her buying trip. She was relieved to see that the diner's phone number was legible on her faded copy of the jukebox receipt. If she didn't press hard enough, the carbonless receipt pad left her with meaningless hieroglyphics. Her finger hovered over the send key after she tapped the number into her phone. What was she going to ask, exactly? *"Excuse me, I'm just curious, but did you sell me an advanced piece of technology designed to mess with my head?"* She decided to ask open-ended questions as if she was just gathering more information about the jukebox.

After the fourth ring, Mac pictured the empty diner, the "back at 6:00" sign hanging in the door. Stan and Moira were in the barn with some other collector, chatting about Christmas kitsch and apple pie. After the fifth ring, Moira's voice came on the line. "You've reached Stan's Diner. Sorry we missed you, but you're just a little too late. The diner will be closed indefinitely until we find someone willing to buy it. Try again next week, if you want." Then came Stan's voice, distant and full of echo. "And Merry Christmas!"

∿

AFTER A LONG NAP and another dose of caffeine, Mac was back in the workshop. She came prepared with a roll of quarters and a clear head. The jukebox was dark and silent again, even though it was securely plugged into the extension cord. It came back to life when Mac unplugged and reconnected it. *I hope it doesn't cost too much to fix that particular glitch,* she thought as she pressed a quarter into the slot. The afternoon dream flitted through her mind for just a second as a record fell into place. Santa flew along his circular path as "Jingle Bells" played. Mac watched and listened for any sign of mechanical

THE CHRISTMAS JUKEBOX

problems. A grinding gear, off-speed turntable, or, heaven forbid, a puff of smoke. She was relieved when the loud but tinny music stopped and Santa's sleigh settled back into home base.

She was about to put in another quarter when she noticed that the display hadn't changed. It still read eleven. Mac smacked the side of the cabinet near the display with her palm. The jukebox went dark again. With a sigh, she un and re-plugged, hoping that it wouldn't just give up completely. It came back to life and Mac dragged the extension cord around to the front of the cabinet to make resetting it easier next time.

Before she could put in another quarter, the jukebox started to play the song again. Santa didn't move, but the red and green lights shined out of the top and flickered on the ceiling. There was something different about the music, too. It was better, Mac thought. Hi-fidelity. Almost too perfect. She peered through the glass front to see if a different record was playing. No record was playing. The turntable was still, but Mac could make out some movement in the bright white light that flooded the middle of the jukebox. The space that used to be the mechanical heart of the machine now began to fill with a diorama like she'd seen before. A small figure appeared but, as Mac strained to see details, the light became brighter and brighter until she had to look away.

She blinked her eyes clear of the red, black, and white dots that overlaid everything she looked at.

"Jingle bells, jingle bells, jingle all the way…"

A burst of sound like rushing wind mixed with the music. Mac turned to see that the light coming from the jukebox had become so bright that she couldn't even look at it from a distance. It rushed from the cabinet, flooding the space in front of it, but did not make it to the far wall. Every ray of light stopped in the middle of the room as if hitting a projection screen.

Goosebumps rose on Mac's arms as the tiny figure she saw inside the jukebox was now a full-sized, glowing, three-dimensional image of a real person. A real person she recognized in a real situation that she remembered. She looked back through time at Richard sitting on his couch, his face lit by the flickering screen Mac knew he was looking at, even though she was between him and the TV. Richard was directly in front of her, looking through her at whatever was playing. He didn't seem to be paying attention, though. In fact, Mac had never seen the expression he was wearing in the vision. His face was slack and his eyes empty. She felt a pang of guilt for intruding on such a private moment. He looked at something off to one side and his face changed almost instantly into the one Mac knew. The sly smile that said he was up for anything took over his mouth and forehead, but not the corners of his eyes. The wrinkles that had recorded thousands of laughs were there, but the ones being formed now angled downward. She would not have noticed it if she hadn't watched the rest of his face transform.

The couch lurched as another person dropped into it next to Richard. Mac stared slack-jawed at herself at Richard's place on movie night about three months ago. She settled into the space under his arm and rested her head against his chest. She flinched as he tugged at her earlobe, and Mac replayed the memory of spilling popcorn even as the jukebox projected it.

As the final "…one horse open sleigh" filled the room, the Mac watching the vision saw Richard's smile dim and make space on his face for the sadness. The Mac in the vision was oblivious. The Mac in the workshop began to cry as the counter slipped to nine.

∼

How had she not known that Richard was going through something? Mac ran their final weeks together through her mind, looking for clues. He'd cancelled a couple of dates at the last minute. The argument in the van on the way back from their last buying trip was not any worse than any of their other disagreements, and they'd made up almost immediately. As she considered it, though, she realized that the argument was different because it wasn't passionate. He had finally just said, "Whatever," and turned up the radio.

The realization hit Mac like a song at full volume. She had lost

Richard long before he left. He was gone even before he started steering money into his account. Mac had not seen what was right before her eyes. She took another quarter from her pocket and slid it into the slot. When it hit bottom, the jukebox prepared itself to play another record.

"Little Drummer Boy" played, first from the speakers and then from the universe. A scene appeared in the belly of the jukebox and then burst into the space in front of Mac.

A handsome man wearing an ugly Christmas sweater faced her from a dozen feet away. He was holding a poorly wrapped gift, apparently offering it to a woman standing between him and Mac. The man was about Mac's age, bearded, and smiling in a way that told Mac that the woman was smiling, too. She was certain she'd never seen him before. The woman was familiar, though. Even though her back was toward Mac, her hair, build, boots, and, most of all, fringed jacket identified her. Mac was looking at herself.

Just as she got possession of herself enough to decide she might be able to walk around the couple to confirm her theory, the music stopped. The lights died and the figures vanished. The room was silent except for the clicking whir of the display changing from nine to eight.

CHAPTER 6

Aaron contemplated the muffin he was carrying in a small brown bag with a green mermaid logo. He'd bought it on a whim when the cashier pointed out the buy one, get one for a dollar deal. The "buy one" muffin had been tasty, but he wasn't thinking about bonus calories when he added the "get one." As the gallery's sign grew big enough to see down the block, Aaron wondered if it might be better to just eat the muffin and get on with his day.

Nicole looked up as the tinkling bells announced his entrance. "Hey, Aaron, what brings you here?"

"Breakfast delivery for Mac." He handed Nicole the paper bag and noticed her puzzled look. "Inside joke. It's just a muffin."

"I'm sure she'll laugh," Nicole said with a poker face which held for exactly four seconds before cracking into a grin. "So, I assume that means you were able to help her yesterday?"

"Yeah. She really didn't need me, and she overpaid, but I was glad to help."

"I kind of talked her into it. She's taking the thing with Richard pretty hard. Closing herself off, you know?"

"Sure. It was a crappy way to end his relationships."

"Have you heard from him at all?"

"No. And I don't expect to. Looking back, I can tell he was easing into buddy land long before he left."

"Buddy land?"

"It's part of my theory of relationships. Guys are strangers until they meet. Then they're acquaintances. If they spend time together, they become buddies. After that comes friends and then best friends. Sometimes it goes the other direction. Most friendships are actually buddyships - trademark Aaron Stiles - and guys spend most of their time in buddy land. They're either more than acquaintances but will never be friends or they were once friends, but something changed."

Nicole looked at Aaron for a few seconds and then said, "You've given this a disturbingly large amount of thought."

Aaron shrugged.

She added, "What about romantic relationships? Is buddy land like the friend zone?"

"I have a whole other theory about women, but we don't have time to go over it. Plus, I'd need my whiteboard and sock puppets."

"Sock puppets?" Mac appeared behind Aaron.

"We were just talking about the mysteries of life," Aaron said as Nicole handed the bag past him to Mac.

"What's this?"

"The breakfast we didn't have yesterday." He suddenly regretted not eating it himself and walking on past the gallery.

"If I'd known we were talking about a Starbucks muffin, I would have taken you up on your offer."

"There might be some crumbs in the bag. And a balled-up napkin. And a receipt. Don't look at the receipt." He held his smile in place until Mac looked up from the bag. She rewarded him with a tired grin.

"Perfect. Thank you. I missed breakfast and this will keep me from pigging out at lunch." She cocked her head as her voice trailed off. "Speaking of lunch, would you like to join me and Nicole as we take a closer look at the jukebox you helped unload? We're trying to figure out where it came from, and I'd appreciate another set of eyes."

He pulled his phone out of his pocket to check the time, even though he knew his day was completely free. "Sure. Why not?"

～

"That is so cool." Nicole squatted in front of the jukebox and peered through the window, her nose practically touching the glass. "I didn't find anything like it online, but it does have a Wurlitzer feel to it."

"That's what I thought, but it doesn't have any markings. That's what makes me think it's a custom piece."

Aaron walked behind the jukebox. "This is interesting. Usually, cabinets have thin, cheap backs because nobody ever sees them. I wouldn't even be surprised to see dense cardboard in a case like this." He gave the back a rap with his knuckle. "But this is real wood. Plywood, probably, but thick and finished like the rest of the cabinet."

"See where a label used to be?"

He knelt and Mac cringed as she imagined the grimy stain his jeans were picking up from the concrete floor. "Yeah. A faded area with two holes where screws used to be. It was probably a metal plate, not a paper label. Too bad it's gone. I'm sure it would have made it easier to determine its provenance."

"Determine its provenance?" The two women said in unison.

"You know, figure out where it came from."

"I know what it means, Aaron. This is my business. I'm just surprised to hear *you* say it," Mac said.

"I must have picked it up from Richard."

After an awkward pause, Mac answered, "I really don't know you, do I?"

Nicole stood facing the jukebox, her arms outstretched as if giving it a hug. She ran her hands along the tubes on each side of the cabinet. "Looks like these are made of glass, not plastic. And thick, too. Do they light up?"

"Yes. The side ones but not the top. It does something else." Nicole stepped aside so Mac could point out the small holes in the arch. "Red and green lights come out here and project onto the ceiling."

THE CHRISTMAS JUKEBOX

"Let's see!"

Mac hesitated. "It's been flakey since I got it back. It worked fine in the diner where I bought it, but something must have wiggled loose on the way here. I'll have to get somebody to look at it."

"Come on, Mac, give it a try." Nicole joined Aaron behind the cabinet and fiddled with the cord. "How do you turn it on?"

"It's always on if it's plugged in. See?" She pointed to the extension cord. "It should be lit up now."

Before Mac could say anything else, Aaron pulled the plug and then reconnected the two cords. Nothing happened. They stood staring at the dark, silent machine for a long minute.

"As interesting as this jukebox is," Nicole said, "Somebody needs to watch the store. Should I go?"

"Sure. Thanks," Mac answered.

After Nicole left, Mac watched Aaron as he continued to examine the jukebox. "Where was this thing? It's in almost perfect shape."

"A diner. Looks like the owners took good care of it. All I've done so far is wipe it down."

"Do you want me to take a look at the guts? I know you've got someone you use for stuff like this, but I really wouldn't mind looking it over."

Mac considered the offer. She didn't know if Aaron had any idea what he was doing, but if there was something odd inside the jukebox, she would rather Aaron find it. For some reason, she trusted this man she had, for all practical purposes, just met. "I guess so, just be super careful. I'm hoping to get a lot of money for it."

"Tools?"

Mac pointed to a cabinet and Aaron rummaged around until returning with a metal toolbox. He unplugged the jukebox and then used a screwdriver to remove the screws holding the rear panel in place, dropping each screw into a baby food jar. "Am I making you nervous?"

"Not really," Mac lied.

"You look nervous. Anyway, most of the stuff I take apart goes back together okay. Usually, there's only a few parts left over." When

Mac didn't answer, Aaron changed tone. "Seriously, it's okay. I built custom computers in high school and then went to work for an HVAC company, installing air conditioners. I'll be careful."

"I trust you."

"Wow. That's interesting." Aaron leaned the back cover gently against the side of the cabinet.

"What?"

"Look how clean it is in here. It's like it just came off the assembly line. But I'm starting to agree with you that this jukebox wasn't made in a factory. Let's see if we can figure out why it doesn't want to stay on."

Mac watched as his fingers moved skillfully along wires, tracing their paths. She knew he wasn't talking to her as he muttered about thermal breakers, Bakelite sockets, and rubber strain relief. After a few minutes of poking around, he sat back and stared into the guts of the machine. Mac asked, "Anything obvious?"

"Not that I can see but I'm not a jukebox expert."

"Anything… weird?"

"This whole thing is kind of weird. Some of the components look modern, but not like anything I've seen before. Other pieces look new but seem to be old technology."

"What about the record player? The mechanical parts."

"Looks like a couple of motors and a bunch of gears. I would have to take the assembly out to see more, and I'm not comfortable doing that."

"Any sort of… projector?"

"Huh?" He stuck his head in and looked up. "No. The lights must come from these bulbs and a couple of motorized mirrors make them dance."

"What about the display? I think it's counting down after every song."

"I saw that. Probably a couple of wheels with motors. The digits from zero to ten are painted on each one and the motor moves them into view." He shifted position. "Let me check one last thing before I button it back up." He reached in with a long screwdriver and came out with a metal box. A long shiny arm protruded from its top. "This is the…"

"Coin box. I know, I've seen those in other units."

"I was going to say 'money thingy' but coin box sounds better." He turned it over in his hands, shook it gently, and dropped a quarter down the chute. "It hitches just a little at the bottom." He pried at the chute with the screwdriver and then slid the assembly back into place. After replacing the back, he held the jukebox plug in one hand and the end of the extension cord in the other. "Ready?"

"Fingers crossed."

The jukebox came to life. Aaron handed Mac the quarter he'd used to test the coin box. "You can have the honors."

Mac held her breath as she put the quarter in the slot. Part of her wanted somebody else to see what she'd seen. Another part still hoped it was all a dream. The coin rattled down the chute, but nothing happened.

Aaron frowned. "I hope I didn't fix one thing and break another."

~

"WE CAN USE THE HELP," Nicole said.

"We can't afford it, though," Mac answered.

"I knew you were going to say that, but I have it all figured out."

"Bank robbery is off the table."

"Well, luckily I have a Plan B." Nicole grinned. "Aaron and I were talking yesterday, finally, you know how quiet he is. Anyway, turns out he's quite handy and not in a 'saw somebody do it on YouTube' way. Not only did he work for the HVAC company, but he was an apprentice finish carpenter."

"Okay…"

"So, what if you have him do some of the work you've been sending out to other shops? Not only could he get items ready to sell but he'd be around to help out with other stuff."

"We send work out for a reason, Nicole. These are professionals.

Richard was no slouch, but even he knew when to call in the pros. I just don't know if Aaron is good enough."

"Why don't you give me a try and find out?" Aaron stuck his head in the door.

"How long have you been here?" Mac asked Aaron while glaring at Nicole.

"Got here just as you were questioning my credentials."

"I didn't tell him to come by, I swear," stammered Nicole. "Why *are* you here?"

"Is that any way to treat your newest employee? Goodness, a hostile work environment and I haven't even started yet." He paused while Mac and Nicole squirmed but couldn't keep a straight face. "Actually, I'm here for the money you are forcing me to take for helping you check out the jukebox. You told me to come in this morning."

"Thirty bucks, right?" Mac didn't wait for confirmation. "Nicole, write Mr..."

"Stiles. Aaron Stiles."

"... Stiles a check for thirty dollars." She turned back to Aaron. "No sense pretending we weren't having that conversation. Do you have the skills to replace any of the shops we use? Before you answer, this isn't a job offer. I'm just asking."

"I have one skill that is pretty rare and is apparently very important to you."

"What's that?"

"I know when I'm in over my head and need to call in someone else. I don't think it would happen often around here... I am pretty good... but you could feel confident that I wouldn't ruin anything because I was too proud." He pushed a lock of hair away from his eye and grinned. "Before you answer, this isn't a job acceptance. I'm just saying."

"Tell you what," Mac said as she handed over the check. "If you are available and willing, you can prep some of the items we haven't sent out yet. You'll be a contractor, not an employee, and this is just a trial. Are you interested?"

"Sure, as long as the hours are flexible. I still need my evening job."

"Should be fine. Nicole can keep you busy when you're here."

As the door to the gallery closed behind Aaron, Nicole said, "It's going to be *really* nice having him around."

"Put it in neutral, girl. We don't want to add sexual harassment to the hostile work environment rap."

"You're no fun."

~

MAC MET the Food Dash gal at the door and traded twenty dollars for her standard burrito combo. Somehow, it always tasted better delivered than in a corner booth at Manny's. She turned a crate on its side in between the recliner and the jukebox. The jukebox glowed and hummed as she laid her dinner out on the crate. She dropped another quarter in the slot, the fourth of the evening. Like the others, it slid down the chute and clattered into the coin box. Santa stirred, the carousel turned, a record fell into place. "Let It Snow" played for two minutes and thirty-six seconds. Red and green lights barely made it to the high ceiling.

At least Aaron hadn't broken anything, although why it didn't respond to the quarter he fed it was still a mystery. What Mac had now was the jukebox she saw, heard, and paid nine hundred dollars for. She didn't have the machine that projected impossibly realistic images of two scenes she recognized and two she didn't.

Aaron said that the jukebox was part old and part new. Maybe the new part was the high-tech system Mac hoped was behind the visions. On the other hand, she thought, a rational answer to how the jukebox made the images only made the other questions harder to answer. How would someone know enough about Mac to create what she saw? Why would they do it? Stan, Moira, and - what's his name - Vic would all have to have been in on it.

Mac strained to recall the term Richard used when she tried to solve the mystery of her rebooting computer. Somebody's razor. Occam's Razor. The simplest explanation is usually the right one. He'd gloated when she realized that the outlet her computer was plugged in to was controlled by the light switch. She had been turning her own machine off at night and back on in the morning. In this case, an elaborate conspiracy involving several people and a holographic jukebox was not the simplest explanation.

That left two possibilities, both of which would make Mr. Occam happy. Mac was sick or Mac was insane.

She finished her rice and fed the jukebox another quarter. "I'll Be Home for Christmas" this time. She kept one eye on the machine as she returned the crate to its place in the corner of the room. If she had been sick, she must be better now. It she had been crazy, it was probably Richard's fault. Time and sleep had returned her to her normal level of sanity, whatever that was. The jukebox was just a jukebox, after all. Mac was going to sell it as quickly as she could, though. Just in case.

~

MAC TURNED on two bright photography lights and aimed them at the jukebox. It looked much less mysterious without the deep and uneven shadows cast by the arch under normal lighting. It almost seemed to be under interrogation. *Where were you on the night of November 10th?*

Richard took all the pictures for the gallery's online catalog, but Mac had been with him most of the time and knew the drill. In fact, she was glad to have the chance. If she was going to have to fill the hole he left, she might as well get to do the fun things, too. She took over a dozen stills, shifting the camera tripod and light stands in a circle around the jukebox after every few shots. She had already turned the lights off when she realized that, unlike most of the items they sold, this collectable didn't just sit there. She adjusted the lights to their lowest output, switched the camera to video mode, and pressed a quarter into the slot. It played "Jingle Bells" again as Mac panned the camera smoothly to capture Santa's sleigh, the record carousel, and the dancing lights.

This was the fifth or sixth time in a row that the jukebox had worked as expected. Mac hadn't even held her breath when the quarter joined its friends in the coin box. Whatever had been going on in the machine, or in her head, was over.

She packed up the photography gear and headed for the door, anxious to get back to her office where she would update the catalog and, hopefully, quickly find a buyer. As she turned off the overhead lights, the soft glow of the jukebox reminded her that it was still plugged in. *It will be alright. It's designed to be on all the time.* She opened the door and then let it swing closed again until stopped by the photography case. *With my luck, some fifty-dollar bulb will burn out, eating into my profit.* She left the lights off, using the wedge of sunlight coming through the door to make her way across the room. She picked up the extension cord where it received the jukebox plug and pulled them apart. She turned back to the door as the machine went dark.

And then it lit up again. Mac took in a sharp breath and kicked the cord as if it were a snake. The plug ended up several feet away from any source of power. Her heart pounded as she moved to the light switch, trying not to panic. The fluorescent overheads flickered to life. The jukebox continued to glow as if Mac hadn't unplugged it.

Curiosity and determination replaced fear as she tugged the last quarter from her jeans.

The coin dropped. The sleigh flew. The record settled onto the turntable and "I'll Be Home for Christmas" began to play, tinny at first but then in the same ultra-Hi-Fi sound as before. Miniature figures appeared behind the window but, before Mac could make them out, they were washed out by a brilliant white light. The light seemed to pass straight through Mac. She turned to see that part of the workshop was now a small, glowing apartment. A man sat on a futon behind a beat-up coffee table. He had a cell phone to his ear, but he wasn't talking. He pulled it away, looked at it briefly, and set it on the table next to a tabletop Christmas tree. He and Mac were looking toward each other, but she knew he wasn't seeing anything. She recognized the look on his face. He was seeing a memory or a regret.

Mac didn't know who he was, but she had seen him before.

After the song ended and the display clicked down to seven, the jukebox fell silent and dark. Mac thought again about Occam's razor and allowed herself to consider what was truly the simplest explanation. The jukebox was exactly what it seemed to be. It was a device that showed Mac things she needed to see. How it worked, where it came from, or why it existed were questions she might never be able to answer. She really only had to answer one question right now: what was she going to do?

The jukebox had shown her a time when she was a happy child. Then it showed her with a man she didn't recognize. A man happy to be with her. Now it had just shown her the same man without her. He was the only mystery. He was the key. He must be what Mac was supposed to see. He must be who Mac is supposed to find.

CHAPTER 7

"What is your deal, Christmas jukebox?" Mac stood with her hands on her hips, staring at the dark and silent machine. "You're plugged in, but then that doesn't seem to matter." She took a quarter from the stack she'd just retrieved from her office and fed it to the jukebox. "Nothing?" She unplugged it, waited a few seconds, and plugged it back in, but nothing happened. "Don't you dare stop right when I decide you're trying to tell me something." She dropped into the recliner, stared up at the ceiling, and listened to the rain as it rushed down the workshop's downspouts. The sudden storm had caught Mac by surprise as she walked from the gallery to the shop. "I'd just give up and leave if I had an umbrella."

Her voice bounced around the space between the concrete floor and high ceiling. The only other sounds were the rain and the faint buzz of the fluorescent lights. "Maybe I am losing my mind. I'm talking to a possessed, oversized music box." As the echoes of her words faded, a new sound joined the others: a familiar hum. Mac popped the recliner into its upright position and looked at the glowing machine. The words *Now, we're cooking* came to her mind but didn't make it out of her mouth. She leaned forward and stared into the window, waiting for something to happen. Then she shook her head, straightened her right leg, and dug in her front pocket for her last quarter. As it landed in the coin box, the machinery behind the window put a record on the turntable. "Let It Snow" began to play, shifting almost immediately to room-filling, perfect sound. Mac didn't even bother looking into the jukebox; she just watched the space next to her chair as it filled with moving lights which coalesced into a moving image.

Her bearded mystery man walked down a city street lined with a few brave trees living in square islands of soil surrounded by sidewalk. He wore a navy jacket but no gloves or scarf. Other people around him were dressed for the cool but not yet cold weather. Mac's view shifted and she watched him come through the door of a Starbucks. She was apparently watching from near the counter but not in the line of customers waiting for their morning - she assumed it was morning - fix. The tone of the music coming from the jukebox changed so that it became part of the background noise of the coffee shop.

Mac took in a deep breath, expecting to smell fresh-brewed coffee and fresh-baked muffins, but the dusty, oily scent of the shop reminded her where she was. Under her breath, Mac said, "Hello, Jukebox Man," as he paid for his coffee and walked toward the front of the shop. He passed so close to Mac that she stepped out of the way, almost expecting him to say, "Excuse me." His eyes were the same shade of brown as his perfectly trimmed beard. As he turned away from her, Mac imagined the air churning around him just enough to send her what she was sure was the subtle scent of a good cologne.

She tried to follow him, but the vision moved away as if it were attached to her. She watched the back of his head move up and down as he sipped his coffee and looked at his phone. A moment of panic gripped her as she noticed that the song was about to end. She looked around for anything that might tell her where she was. Just as the music began to fade, she looked through the coffee shop's front window. The frame hid all but two letters of the big sign across the street, but they were enough to identify the store. A giant VS told her she was in a Starbucks across the street from a CVS drug store.

THE CHRISTMAS JUKEBOX

"Bingo!"

"Bingo, what?" Nicole asked from the other room.

"Never mind," Mac said without looking away from her computer. "Just talking to myself."

"Let me know when I should listen."

Mac zoomed in on the map of downtown Kansas City until two dots filled the center of the screen. Starbucks and CVS weren't exactly across the street, but close enough that you might be able to see one through the window of the other. Mac also wondered how exact the visions were. The one from her childhood, for instance, showed a couch she was pretty sure the family never owned.

As exciting as it was to find a place that might lead her to Mr. Jukebox, or J.B., as she now thought of him, Mac knew there might be more than one match. Maybe many more. "Hey, Nicole." Nicole didn't budge. With an eye roll, Mac added, "Ms. Nicole, now is a good time to listen."

"Ah. What can I do for you, Boss?"

"I have a weird lead on an antique store. Do you have time to help solve a mystery?"

Nicole was rubbing her hands together when she walked into Mac's office. "I *always* have time for a good mystery."

"The guy I talked to didn't have an address for this magical store. He cruises around a lot like I do. He just said it was near a Starbucks and a CVS."

"Here in Sloan?"

"That's where the real mystery part comes in. If he said the name of the city, I didn't write it down."

"Can't you just call him?"

"I just ran into him and didn't get his contact info." Mac decided to narrow Nicole's search so she wouldn't ask any more questions. "We were talking about our neck of the woods so it's most likely within a day's drive." *If it's much further than that, I'll never find J.B. Anyway.*

49

"So, I'm looking for an antique shop near both a Starbucks and a CVS within, what, 400 miles?"

"Focus on the Starbucks and CVS. The place we're looking for could be a store, a gallery, or even a thrift shop."

Nicole went to work searching the states neighboring the top half of Texas. Mac scanned the CVS store directory, noting the ones in places where the weather was still mild in November but had trees like the ones in the vision. No palm or pine trees. As the cities scrolled up the screen, she pushed her mouse away and rested her head on her folded arms. There had to be hundreds of matching locations and she would have to check every one against the Starbucks list. Nicole must have made the same connection. She said, "Are you sure this place is worth it? There are a lot of stores to sift through."

"It's worth it. I desperately need to find that... store."

~

ANOTHER TWO DOLLARS' worth of quarters had not coaxed the jukebox into showing Mac another vision. She had hoped to get more clues about where J.B lived. Instead, she was now arriving in Wichita Falls after a two-hour drive. It was the closest address on Nicole's list. She was still skeptical and made Mac promise to stop at a couple of other places to make the trip worthwhile. "We're running on borrowed money, which means we're running on borrowed time," she'd said.

Mac's grip on the wheel loosened as she traded the huge, busy freeway for quieter neighborhood roads. Her phone warned her too late about her final turn, so she had to go around the block before laying eyes on the two landmarks she was looking for. The coffee shop and drug store were a hundred yards apart. It could not be the right place.

"Hey, Nicole," Mac said to the phone attached to the dash. "Looks like I'm going on to San Antonio."

"No magical antique store, huh?"

"Not unless it's also invisible. What have you got for me between here and there?"

"Hold on… let's see… a bunch of stores and galleries popped up around Waco. That's on your way."

"It has been a while since I've been to Fixer Upper land. I'm guessing that there aren't many cheap hidden treasures left in Chip and Joanna's neck of the woods, but I'm willing to check it out."

Mac did visit one thrift shop just so she didn't have to lie to Nicole, but her heart wasn't in it. She even bought a metal Dr. Pepper sign with what the owner said was a bullet hole in it. Mac had her doubts but would pass the legend on to whoever ended up giving her twice what she paid for it.

She spent the three hours behind the wheel wondering how she was ever going to find J.B. and what she would say when she did.

∼

By population, San Antonio the bigger city, but Dallas feels bigger. It is the spider in the web of concrete cloverleafs that make up the Dallas-Fort Worth metroplex. As much as Mac despised traffic, she didn't mind moving around San Antonio. For one thing, it didn't take nerves of steel and the reflexes of a New York City cabbie to drive downtown. She quickly found the coffee shop and drug store. They were separated by two lanes and a wide median. The only empty parking spot was too small for the van, so Mac took another turn around the block and parked in a small public garage. As she walked toward the stairs, she noticed that she wasn't too far from the Starbucks and could see the CVS. Her pulse quickened as she leaned over the barrier to look at the people moving back and forth along the sidewalks, enjoying a nearly perfect November day in Texas. *Are you down there somewhere?*

One of the urban trees from the vision greeted her as she emerged from the garage. It was bigger than she remembered, but had plenty of friends of slightly different sizes along the walks and in the median. Hope that she was in the right place mixed with doubt that the she would find it so easily so soon.

A Texas gentleman held the door to the coffee shop for her. It was a typical Starbucks, and Mac walked to the space near the register where she had stood in the vision. A woman scowled as she had to go out of her way to avoid Mac. "Excuse me," Mac said as she replayed the similar interaction with J.B. *This could be it.* She ordered a latte and took a seat at the bar-height counter facing the front window. The view didn't exactly match the vision, but she could see the CVS store and sign across the street. *This really could be it.*

The shop was nearly empty when Mac arrived, but traffic increased as exhausted office workers stopped in for their second wind on their way home. She wasn't completely up to speed on her coffee shop etiquette, but knew she could sit there for quite a while before qualifying as a squatter. Being seen as a stalker was a different thing, so she tried to be as subtle as she could as she examined every bearded face that came through the door. She was afraid that J.B. would get past her if the vision wasn't perfect or current. What if he had shaved off the beard? What if his eyes were not exactly the shade she remembered?

Three hours, one latte, a muffin, and a smoothy later, Mac left the shop confident that she hadn't missed him. She was also pretty sure that this was, or at least could be, the place. Even with the coffee buzz still working, Mac knew it was too late for her to start the long drive back home, especially if she was just going to turn around and come back to look for J.B.

It took more than thirty minutes to get far enough out of the city to find a safe, inexpensive motel. She checked in with Nicole, ate the other half of her lunch sandwich, and went to bed early. *I want to be the early bird tomorrow.*

∼

RATHER THAN EVEN TRY TO FIGHT FOR street parking, Mac parked in the same spot in the same garage as the day before. She slung her messenger bag over her shoulder so she would have her computer to make her stakeout look less obvious. The bright overhead lights made the city outside seem dark, even as the sun came up behind what passed for skyscrapers in San Antonio. As she emerged from the protection of the building and onto the street, a gentle but consistent cool breeze almost made her regret not wearing a jacket. She knew, though, that any extra layer she had with her would, in fifteen minutes, become extra baggage for the rest of the day. The Texas sun had a way of turning sixty into eighty degrees, even in the middle of November.

She looked up from the bag strap she was adjusting. Half a block ahead and lit by a streetlight that went out for the day just as he walked beneath it was a bearded man dressed like J.B. in the vision. He turned away from Mac and walked toward the coffee shop. Mac's breaths came faster than her increased pace called for as she made up the distance. *What do I even say?* She decided to make sure it was him before determining her next move. Acting as if in a hurry to get somewhere, Mac brushed past the man, bumping him with her bag. "Excuse me," she said.

The man with the too-long beard and wrong-colored eyes said, "No problem," without even looking at Mac. He continued past the Starbucks, so Mac went in and bought a coffee. While the barista did her thing, Mac looked around the crowded shop looking for J.B. It occurred to her that the store only had one way in and out. She took her coffee to go and went back outside.

Across the street and in front of the drug store was a metal bench with an ad for a law firm covering most of its back. Mac made her way across the street and sat down, having the bench all to herself. She sipped at her coffee and pretended to look at her phone while watching people come and go through the Starbucks door. The shop was busy, but she was sure nobody had made it past her.

After the morning rush, Mac had time to relax a little and enjoy the magic window between chilly and muggy. Even the smells of the city changed as the sun rose higher in the sky. She could make out the scents of flowers and breakfasts and the subtle perfume of the woman who sat next to her for a minute. Once the concrete and asphalt started to warm up, the subtler smells had trouble making it through.

As she looked around, she compared more carefully what she saw with what she remembered from the vision. The stores weren't aligned exactly how she recalled, but the CVS sign was visible from the Starbucks and the trees matched. But something wasn't quite right. It nagged at her, preventing her from being sure she was looking for the right man in the right place. She watched a cyclist swerve into the reserved lane, prompting a curse and unprofessional gesture by the driver of the bus he'd just cut off. She closed her eyes and remembered the vision. *Trains, not busses.*

With a sigh, Mac got up and told herself that her time on a bench in San Antonio hadn't been a complete waste of time. She had enjoyed a nice fall morning and a good cup of coffee, the caffeine of which would get her started on her half day of driving home.

CHAPTER 8

"You're not Nicole."

"Neither are you," Aaron replied.

"Is everything okay? Where is Nicole?" Mac pictured Nicole away having a manicure while Aaron, someone Mac barely knew, manned the gallery.

"It's all good. I don't know exactly where she is, but she's close enough I could hear her yell 'Can you get that?' at the top of her lungs. Should I go get her?"

"No, I just wanted to let her know that I didn't find what I was looking for and I'm headed back."

"No luck in the treasure hunt, huh?"

"Treasure hunt?"

"Nicole said you are searching for hidden treasure."

"Was an eye roll involved?"

"As a new kind-of employee, I think it best that I not answer that question."

"Uh, huh. Anyway, please ask Nicole to add light rail to the list. She'll know what I mean."

"Yes, Ma'am. Anything I can do to help? I love a puzzle."

"Thanks, but I think we've got it under control. Just fix up whatever Nicole asks you to work on. We really need to turn some inventory."

"Speaking of inventory, I've been poking around in that jukebox a little bit, and..."

"Don't!" Mac leaned toward the dash as if Aaron were in the holder next to her phone. "Sorry. Didn't mean to shout. Just leave the jukebox alone until we know a little more about it. I still have no idea how much it might be worth, and we don't want to do anything to reduce its value."

Aaron's reply was so quiet that Mac had to ask him to repeat it. "I was very careful. It's exactly the way you left it."

"Okay. Sorry. I'm just frustrated."

"No problem." Aaron's volume was almost back to normal. "I'm sure you'll find what you're looking for, eventually."

"I sure hope so."

He must think I've lost my mind. A brief rush of resentment set Mac's jaw and colored her cheeks. Even if Aaron turned out to be useful, he was an unnecessary complication. She wondered how she had ever let Nicole bring Aaron into the picture. *After the way I just talked to him, maybe the problem will solve itself.*

∼

Mac half expected to find the gallery closed and dark. They often closed a few minutes early during the week, especially on slow days. When she came in the back door at exactly closing time, the lights were all on and Nicole was just locking the front door. She jumped when Mac said, "Hey."

"You're back." She hurried to Mac and steered her into the office. "You need to talk to Aaron."

"Already? What has he or you done?"

"It's not like that. He was a little off after talking to you on the phone. When he came back from the workshop an hour later, he was sort of freaked out."

"Is he here?"

"Back at the shop. I could tell he didn't want to, but he told me to ask you to stop by."

"Any idea what's going on? I wasn't really planning on doing anything other than dropping the van off, but I guess I can take the sign I bought out to the shop. Maybe Aaron can clean it up for us. That is, if he isn't about to quit."

∼

THE LOOK on Aaron's face when he met her at the door made Mac think her sarcastic prediction might have been right. "What's up?"

"I am so sorry."

Mac tilted her head in a 'For what?' gesture.

"After we talked about the jukebox, I wanted to make sure it really was in the same shape as when you left." They walked together and stood facing it. "I think I broke it."

Mac took a deliberate breath but couldn't keep her voice as level as she wanted. "What do you mean, 'broke it'?"

"Here. I'll show you." He slid a quarter into the slot. When it hit the bottom, everything happened as expected until a record settled onto the turntable. It turned but played no music. After a couple of minutes, the mechanical arm retrieved the record and returned it to its place in the carousel. Aaron said, "I'm so sorry. I don't know what I did, but it must be my fault, right?"

"Give me another quarter." An unexpected calm came over Mac as she tested the theory that had just occurred to her. As Santa flew and a record started to play, she didn't know whether she hoped for a normal song or for Aaron to become witness to a vision.

When the normal Christmas jukebox finished playing a slightly scratchy version of "Silver Bells", Mac said quietly, "It only works for me."

"What do you mean?"

"It's obviously a magical jukebox meant just for me," she said, hoping she sounded sarcastic. When Aaron's expression didn't change, she added, "You know how it goes. It's like when you take your car to the mechanic. It never makes the noise when he drives it."

"But it worked, then I fiddled with it, and then it didn't work."

"And then it worked again. Really. Don't worry about it."

"But you can't sell it like that, can you? What if it glitches a day or a week after somebody pays a lot of money for it?"

"Don't worry about it."

"How about if I…"

"Aaron. Seriously. It's most likely working exactly like it's supposed to. Go home."

She didn't think it was possible, but Aaron's face fell even further as he walked toward the storage room. "I'm parked out this way. Okay if I cut through storage?"

"Sure." She forced a smile. "See you tomorrow?"

"Uh, huh. Open or shut?" He held the storeroom door halfway between the two options.

"Closed. Thanks."

After he left, Mac put in another quarter and dropped herself into the recliner while the coin dropped into the coin box. "What's your deal, jukebox," she asked. It answered by playing, in perfect fidelity, the most beautiful version of "Silver Bells" that anyone had ever heard. Brilliant light erupted from the jukebox just as the title phrase filled the room. *The light isn't actually white, it's more of a silver,* Mac thought. Light within light formed the vision in front of her. She had to squint to be sure that the jukebox was showing a vision of itself. It was in a small space showing something to a single viewer. "What the?" Mac said aloud as she watched herself watch the jukebox while sitting on the floor of her van. "What did you just show me?"

The counter on the jukebox changed to five.

Aaron took his hand off the knob on the other side of the storeroom door and silently left the building.

∼

AARON SAW the van idling in front of the gallery with its flashers on. He had a cup of coffee in each hand, one for him and one for Nicole. He wasn't expecting Mac to be in so early, but there she was, holding the door for him.

"Good morning," they said in unison.

"Coffee?" Aaron extended one hand toward Mac and the other toward Nicole, who was standing nearby.

"Thanks," Mac answered. "You just saved me a stop."

"Sorry again about the jukebox."

"No. It's okay. I'm sorry for snapping at you."

"So we're good? I was afraid I was going to have to clean out my non-existent desk today."

"Only if Nicole fires you." Mac's smile emptied her threat. "See you later. Call me if you need me, Nicole."

Aaron heard himself say, "What if *I* need you?"

"You won't." That smile again.

After the door closed behind Mac, Nicole took the other cup from Aaron and said, "Ouch. That's going to leave a mark."

"Yeah. I don't even know where that came from. Bartending occupational hazard, I guess. You don't think she thinks I meant anything by it, do you?"

"Probably not, but you never know. It was good to see her smile, though. Haven't had much of that lately."

"Glad to be of service. Speaking of which, I need to head out for a bit."

"Already? You just got here."

"First, I need a coffee. Second, I need to look at a few pieces in the shop, so I know what supplies and materials I'll need."

"You gave Mac your coffee. How gallant."

Aaron ignored the comment and opened the door. "I'll be back soon."

When he paid for his coffee - again, he told the keypad he wanted five dollars cash back. "Could I get two of those dollars in quarters?"

He wasn't sure what secrets Mac and the jukebox were keeping, but he was suddenly and inexplicably determined to find out. He was not going to take it apart again, he'd learned that lesson, but maybe he missed something when he looked at it before. He now had eight chances to see if he could get it to play the perfect music he heard the night before.

The shop door was locked, and Aaron spilled his coffee as he searched his pockets for the key. He was halfway across the floor, muttering and patting at his pants, before he finally looked toward the jukebox.

It was gone.

~

WHILE HE MADE the list of materials he'd used as his excuse to go to the shop in the first place, Aaron puzzled over the jukebox. Mac had obviously taken it with her, but unless she had asked someone besides Aaron or Nicole to help her, she had loaded it herself. Aaron found it odd that Mac would panic about doing anything to reduce its value, but then risk strapping it to a dolly and muscling it up a ramp and into the van.

"Are you sure Mac didn't say anything about the jukebox?" Aaron asked Nicole when he got back to the gallery.

"Yeah. Why?"

"It's gone. She must have taken it with her. Maybe she found a buyer?"

"I don't think so. She would have mentioned it."

"So, she is on... what did you call it... her 'treasure hunt'?"

A look of confusion melted into a sheepish grin. "I don't call it that to her face. She is obsessed with finding an antique shop that some guy told her about. We spent hours on the Internet looking for it."

"Any luck?"

"She's already been halfway across Texas but, no. Nothing yet. All she has to go on is that the place is supposed to be near both a Starbucks and a CVS drug store."

"There still have to be dozens of possibilities."

"Over a hundred unless you narrow it down to cities within a day's drive and where the Starbucks and CVS are within a block of each other."

"Maybe the guy told her something that makes her think she can sell the jukebox at this mystery store," Aaron speculated.

"Could be. We should know one way or another in a couple of hours." Nicole looked at her phone. "She should be about a third of the way to Oklahoma City by now."

"Be honest. Do you get a weird vibe from that jukebox or the way it's affecting Mac?"

Nicole answered, "Not really. She's been acting a little strangely the past couple of days, but I still blame Richard. She's recovering from him bailing on her while, at the same time, trying to salvage their business."

Nicole sounded like she was looking for a partner for a round of Richard-bashing, but Aaron had other priorities. He said, "I wish I knew more about the jukebox. I'd like to restore it so Mac can get as much as possible out of it."

"If she doesn't sell it today."

"Right. Who'd she buy it from?"

"Some diner a couple hundred miles west of here. The receipt should be in my file by now but, knowing Mac, it's probably somewhere in the mess on her desk." Nicole got up and Aaron followed her into Mac's office. Nicole sifted through the top layer of a pile that looked like it had already been searched by a burglar in a hurry. "That didn't take long." She brandished the back page of a No Carbon Required receipt as if she were the triumphant burglar.

Aaron took it and noticed where Mac had overwritten the phone number. "Looks like she might have already called them."

Nicole headed for the door. "As much as I love this mystery, I have to run a couple of errands. Can you watch things and answer the phone if it rings?"

After Nicole left, Aaron dialed the number on the receipt and got a message about the diner being closed. He was formulating a response in his mind when a robotic voice told him the mailbox was full. He examined the receipt again and could barely make out the name of the diner. The first name of the seller was too faded to read, but it was short and followed by what Aaron was pretty sure was the last name of Caldwell. If the diner was named after the owner, his name was Stan Caldwell.

Aaron sat in Mac's chair and used her computer to search the Internet. Fifteen minutes later, he'd learned that all three of Stan's Diner's Yelp reviews were positive, that a Stanley Caldwell lived at an address two digits away from the diner, and that he had a phone number different from the one on the receipt. Aaron dialed it.

∼

"Hello, this is Stan."

"Hi. My name is Aaron Stiles. I work for Mac Talley. She bought a jukebox from you, I believe."

"Sure. Mac. Sweet gal. She sure fell for the Christmas jukebox. They were made for each other."

"Have you spoken to her since she was at your place?"

"No, is she okay?" Stan sounded more worried than Aaron would expect a one-time customer to be.

"She's fine. I'm just following up for her and didn't want to bother you if you've already talked."

"Who are you, again?"

"Aaron Stiles. Mac hired me recently to help her get items ready to sell."

"She's not selling the jukebox already, is she?"

"I don't think so. Not yet. She asked me to clean it up and see what I could learn about its history."

"Is it working okay? It can be a little persnickety."

"That's good to hear, actually. All of its components seem to be working great, but it does refuse to play music sometimes. I was afraid I had broken it."

Stan chuckled. "I wouldn't worry too much as long as you don't take a sledgehammer to it. That machine is too stubborn to give in to a little tinkering."

"If Mac is going to sell it to a collector, it might need more than a little tinkering to fully restore it. Do you have any documentation for it? I searched online for a service manual or installation guide but couldn't find anything."

"You won't find anything online or anywhere, for that matter. The Christmas jukebox is one of a kind."

"Custom built?"

"You could say that. So, Aaron, right?"

"That's right."

"So, Aaron, is Mac happy with her purchase? I'll give her a full refund if she wants to return it."

"As far as I know, she's satisfied. In fact, she seems..." Aaron recalled being snapped at. "... protective."

"That's good. Protective is a great way to put it."

After an awkward few seconds, Aaron said. "Well, thank you for your time."

"You're welcome, Son. Oh, and Aaron, will you give Mac a message?"

"Happy to."

"Tell her not to give up on that old machine. It's worth a lot more in her hands than in somebody's basement or gallery. And tell her to call us if they need us."

CHAPTER 9

Oklahoma City looked like the right place before Mac was anywhere near the Starbucks. While other drivers seemed annoyed to have to wait for a lime green train to go by, Mac smiled. She didn't even make a confirmation pass before parking in the first open spot and walking toward the coffee shop. Her head swiveled back and forth as she ticked off the items from the vision. Trees, check. CVS, check. Starbucks, check. Train tracks, check. J.B., not yet. It was between breakfast and lunch, so pedestrian traffic was light. Mac was able to eliminate every person on the sidewalk as a potential J.B.

Nobody was in line waiting for coffee, and only a couple of tables were occupied. Mac wasn't ready for another coffee, so she bought a smoothie and set up shop near the front window. She angled her laptop so she could look over its screen out into the street and, with a slight turn of her head, at the door. As long as she didn't get distracted by actually using the computer, there was no way she could miss J.B. if he passed by or came into the shop. She felt self-conscious just sitting there, alternately surfing the web for a minute and then staring into space. She wondered if she should look for a place across the street where she could watch without looking like a vagrant. As she got up to stretch, she noticed a woman across the room hunched over her laptop, typing furiously. Suddenly, she stopped, looked at the ceiling, and scribbled something on a legal pad. After a minute, she began banging away at her keyboard again.

A writer! Her problem solved, Mac mimicked the woman, pretending to write the next Great American Novel. At first, she typed "The quick brown fox jumped over the lazy dog" over and over but soon became worried that someone would come up behind her and see her screen. She opened a new document and typed, "Vision One." As long as she was pretending to write, she might as well document what the jukebox had shown her so far.

She looked up often enough to be confident she hadn't missed J.B. but writing about the visions was becoming more than just a disguise. As she recalled and recorded them, a pattern emerged. She saw herself and then J.B. Then she saw them together. The first visions were of the past. The latest were of the future. Only the one with Richard in it didn't seem to fit. She finished reviewing what she'd written so far and absently reached for her smoothie. It was empty. Just like the last three times she had picked it up and decided not to get another. This time, she put the cup in the trash and went to the counter for a tall coffee.

Her mind had already shifted from buying coffee back to contemplating jukeboxes when she turned too quickly toward her table and bumped full force into the person behind her in line. Coffee escaped onto Mac's jacket through the lid's small opening. The rest of the top stayed in place, preventing a very awkward first meeting.

"So sorry," Mac said as she ignored the small dark spot on her jacket. She Looked up, instead, to see how far the liquid had flown and just how sorry she was going to be.

"No problem. Looks like I escaped unscathed."

Mac opened her mouth to answer but couldn't make any sound. J.B. was handing her a stack of napkins from the nearby dispenser. She finally managed to say, "Umm, good. Sorry again."

J.B. smiled politely, looked up at the menu, and then ordered a cappuccino. Her heart pounded as if she had downed the coffee in her hand in a single gulp. Mac took a step back while still staring at the man of her visions. He looked exactly like the jukebox had revealed. But now she had a smooth, confident voice to go with the picture. And a smell. Probably not cologne but the mid-day remnants of a body wash or even shampoo.

Like a dog who found itself with a tire in its mouth, Mac panicked at the thought of catching what she'd been chasing. She walked back toward her table to collect herself and saw her own reflection in the window. Her face was still red from the encounter and her hair had come half free from the pen she'd used to hold it out of the way while she typed. The new stain on her vintage jacket completed a nearly perfect image of the type of person that might hang out in a coffee shop all day. *What a great first impression, Mac.*

She hurriedly packed up her computer and, at a discreet distance, followed J.B. out the door. As they walked down the same sidewalk, Mac cursed herself for not being better prepared for this moment. J.B. looked over his shoulder to check traffic before crossing the street and Mac felt his eyes linger on her from behind his sunglasses. She panicked and spun around, bumping right into her second man of the day.

"So sorry. Excuse me."

"No worries," said Aaron.

~

IT TOOK Mac a second to process the fact that Aaron was the man she had just bumped into. He was taking a step back and raising his hands in a 'let me explain' gesture while she recovered. She asked the obvious question with her narrowing brow and piercing eyes.

Aaron answered. "I was in the neighborhood."

"Uh, huh."

"Really. I have a friend who lives just outside of town. We've been meaning to get together for months. When Nicole mentioned you were here on your quest, I figured I could kill two birds with one stone."

"Which two birds are you planning to murder?" Mac sounded angrier than she was. Aaron was receiving some of the frustration she felt about blowing her first encounter with J.B.

"The visit with my friend, obviously, and a chance to help you find that antique shop."

"And you just happened to be walking down this street at this moment."

"Actually, yes. At least the 'at this moment' part. I knew which street to try because of the Starbucks and the CVS."

"I see that Nicole gave you the whole story."

"I don't know about that. She told me about the detective work she was doing for you." He pretended not to notice that Mac was about to speak. "Speaking of detective work… I did a little of my own."

"I can't wait to hear this." Mac's eyes softened and Aaron relaxed in response.

"Step into my office." He gestured toward the coffee shop.

He ushered her to the table she had been sitting at just a few minutes earlier. She'd had enough coffee for the day but was glad that Aaron went to the counter to buy one for himself. She needed the time to sort through the thoughts and emotions hammering at her brain and tear ducts. She looked at Aaron expectantly as he settled into the seat across from her. He said, "I've been looking into the jukebox. Not actually *looking into it*, as in taking it apart again. I learned my lesson on that one. But then you know I didn't open it up because you have it with you." Mac held a poker face. "Right?"

"Right. I, um, the store owner is supposedly a jukebox expert. I thought he might be able to help me appraise it," Mac said, trying to keep track of the story she was weaving on the fly.

"That makes sense. Well, I talked to the guy you bought if from."

"Stan?"

"Yep. It was a strange conversation. He didn't tell me anything very useful except that it is a custom piece. Other than that, he talked about it like it was more of a person than a machine. Oh, and he said you could have a refund if you want to return it but that you shouldn't give up on it."

"What do you mean, 'he talked about it like it was a person'?"

"He said it was stubborn and that you two were meant for each other. Like I said, it was a strange conversation."

"But I shouldn't give up on it."

"Right. So, any luck finding this store?"

"Not yet." Mac tried to skirt the truth without lying. "I'm in the right city, though. I'll come back tomorrow if I don't find it on my way out of town. I don't like to drive when I'm tired, so I need to get going."

"Hold on a second." Aaron began tapping furiously on his phone. He smiled at a response and tapped his reply. "I just saved you six hours of driving, tired or not."

"What?"

"Kelly, my friend, says you can stay with her. With us." He blushed. "Not with us but at her place."

"No..."

Aaron interrupted. "Wait. Kelly has a ranch just outside the city. She rents rooms in the main house, an old bunkhouse, and a couple of cabins. It's pretty quiet between now and Christmas, so she has space."

"I appreciate the offer, but I'm good to drive back."

"And forth? Come on, Mac, you'll love this place." He looked down at her cowboy boots. "You'll fit right in."

Mac pictured herself behind the wheel of the van late in the evening and then again before dawn in the morning. Then she compared that with the thought of climbing into a comfortable bed after what was bound to be an awkward evening with Aaron and his friend. She sighed. "Fine, if you're sure it's okay with your friend."

"It's more than fine. She gets desperate for company when the place is empty. Plus, I can help you in your search tomorrow."

Mac suddenly wished she had chosen option A.

∽

THE VAN PULLED up to the main house of Starcrest Ranch, followed closely behind by the trail of dust it stirred up from the long gravel driveway. The trip had been short and quiet. Country music played softly, punctuated every few minutes by Aaron's directions. As soon as the dust settled and they opened their doors to get out of the van, a tall, tan, Amazonian princess came out to meet them. As she got closer to the van, Mac realized that her bearing and embroidered red cowboy boots made her appear taller than she was. Still, when she and Aaron embraced, their heads fit perfectly next to each. Mac watched through the van's windows as Kelly kissed Aaron on the cheek. She couldn't tell if that was her original target or if he had turned his head at the last minute. When Mac came around the van, Kelly had her hand on Aaron's arm as she listened intently to his description of the trip.

"This is Mac. Mac, meet Kelly."

Kelly extended her hand and waited while Mac adjusted her backpack to free hers. "Glad to meet you, Mac. Welcome to Starcrest Ranch."

"Pleased to meet you, too. And thanks for having me." Mac resisted the urge to stare at Kelly's hair. When Kelly turned her head, Mac glanced down to discover that hair and boots were the same shade of red.

"Happy to help. It's nice to have some new company, too. I hate it when the place is empty." She winked at Mac while addressing Aaron. "So, is Mac my competition?"

She couldn't be sure, but Mac thought she saw the tips of Aaron's ears turn red. He said, "The race is over, Kel. But thanks for the bump into the wall."

Kelly dug two keys out of her back pocket. Instead of a cheap piece of plastic with a room number printed on it, each key was attached to a metal disc. Below the hole where, Mac assumed, it would hang from a hook while waiting for the next guest, was a room number engraved in ornate script. Mac fingered hers as Kelly placed it in her hand. "This is gorgeous."

"Thanks," Kelly answered with a humble smile.

"She made those," Aaron added. "That's her thing. Well, one of her things. Metal art."

"It reminds me that I'm not just a glorified night clerk at the Motel 6." She pointed back down the driveway. "You passed four cabins on your way up here. Wait." She made a swapping gesture with her hands. "Swap keys. Mac might be more interested in number 4's decor than you, Aaron. Get yourselves settled. Dinner's at six here in the dining room."

Kelly was right about the furnishings piquing Mac's interest. They were a mix of cowboy kitsch, genuine antiques, and Kelly's artwork. A lamp just inside the door was most interesting. It had no shade. Behind the bare bulb was the silhouette of a face in profile, a ten-gallon hat tilted forward as if the person was sleeping. When Mac turned on the light, the front of the lamp bathed the entry in a warm glow while the back cast a life-size shadow on the opposite wall.

She tugged off her boots and stretched out on the bed, hoping for a catnap. She was tired enough to doze off, but the events of the day got to her before sleep did. Richard, J.B., Aaron, and, for some reason, Kelly took turns chasing away the drowsiness. She didn't even know she'd fallen asleep until her phone woke her up.

CHAPTER 10

There was no sign of Aaron when Mac came out of her cabin a few minutes before six, so she walked alone toward the main house. Her feet on the gravel made the only sounds until she approached a patio she hadn't noticed earlier. A male voice said something she couldn't hear, and a female voice laughed heartily. Then they reversed roles and Mac recognized the tone of Aaron's voice in his laugh. They were still smiling when Mac walked through the cast iron gate set in a low stone wall. "Hey, Mac."

"Evening," Mac answered.

"How do you like your cabin?" Kelly gestured to a chair by pushing a basket of tortilla chips toward it. Aaron moved from the bench he had been sharing with Kelly to a chair across the table from her. Mac ended up at the point of a triangle with Aaron to her right and Kelly to her left.

"It's awesome. I loved the sculptures, especially the lamp. All yours?"

"Yes. Thanks. I'm glad you liked it."

"We normally only show antiques and collectibles in our... my gallery, but I'd love to put something of yours on the floor if you're willing."

"That's tempting but no, I don't do it for money. I'm afraid that the fun will die the first time I try to please someone else."

Mac nodded as if she understood and put a chip in her mouth to avoid saying something wrong. Over a wonderful, authentic Mexican dinner, Kelly explained how she decided not to sell the ranch she'd inherited from her father and how she regretted the decision about half the time. Although her confidence and good looks still intimidated Mac somewhat, she couldn't help liking Kelly and finally felt comfortable asking the question. "How do you know Aaron?"

"We learned how to weld together. He likes to say that, when we met, sparks flew."

Aaron shook his head. "A bad pun can outlive any relationship, apparently."

"Come on Aaron, 'What a MiG torch joineth, let no man put asunder.'"

"You are the only person I know who can out dad-joke my dad." Aaron turned to Mac. "The HVAC company I worked for sent me to school to learn how to braze and weld so I could be more useful to them. Kelly had grown bored with her privileged life of luxury and was looking for a hobby."

Kelly launched a chip like a Ninja throwing star, hitting Aaron in the cheek. "I had just started making art out of metal and had learned as much as I was going to from the welding rig's manual and YouTube. The class had an odd number of students, and I was happy to be the only one not paired with someone else. Then Aaron appeared."

He took over the story. "I thought the universe was finally making up for the string of bad luck I'd been having. I walk in the door a couple days after class officially started, and the instructor says, 'I guess you're partnered up with Kelly there.' She was sweaty and dirty and didn't take her welding glove off when she shook my hand. But she was the prettiest girl I'd been within fifty feet of…"

"… Because of the restraining order," Kelly interrupted.

"… in, well, ever." Aaron's attempted chip retaliation missed wide right.

THE CHRISTMAS JUKEBOX

"Sounds romantic," Mac said.

"It was. For a while it was really romantic." Kelly's smile faded from broad to melancholy. "Then I broke it. Been trying to fix it ever since." She stood and collected the dinner plates. "On that note, I am going to leave you two alone. I've got to finish a thing before tomorrow. Kimi is coming in the morning. She'll take care of the rest of these dishes and make us breakfast. You won't want to miss it. Seven sharp." She paused with dishes stacked on both hands, waitress style. "You know the cliche about relationships ending with 'We can still be friends'? Well, Aaron can."

After the door closed behind Kelly, Mac moved to the chair across from Aaron. She said, "She's got a 'thing' to finish? What was that all about?"

"Who knows. She's always been a tough one to figure out."

"You don't think she thinks we're together, do you?"

Stone-faced, Aaron answered, "We're not?"

"Too bad she took the chips. I'm pretty good in a food fight."

"I told her I work for you and that I was here trying to help you out. Kelly's going to think what Kelly's going to think, though."

"I think she still has a thing for you."

"I think you might be right. She's been trying to coax me back this direction ever since my sister passed away."

"Oh, goodness, Aaron. I didn't know. I'm sorry for your loss."

"Thanks. It's been a tough year, but life gets a little easier every day."

"You came to Sloan for your sister?"

"Yeah. She moved there to, as she put it, 'get some space but not too much'. She was already sick, and moving didn't make her any better. I came to help but her disease got her anyway. That's the story." His tone and tired features told Mac it was all of that story she was going to get.

"So, Kelly wants you back, huh? Are you tempted?"

"Some days. I do like being around her. As you probably noticed, she is full of life. She's also a little flakey."

"How so?"

"It's sort of like the Richard situation. Everything seemed to be going great and then he disappeared, right? Well, imagine that instead of vanishing, he showed up at your place with a girl on his arm and was shocked that you got upset. That's how Kelly ended our relationship."

"And you still speak to her?"

"Not for a long time. But now I get her. And I think she's changed some, too." Aaron stared at Mac for a long second before adding, "Would you still speak to Richard if you got the chance?"

She looked away. "Probably." She smiled as she turned back toward Aaron. "If for no other reason than to ream him out."

They laughed and then enjoyed a comfortable silence. Aaron broke it by saying, "What's the plan for tomorrow?"

"I plan to find the guy who can tell me about the jukebox. You have the day off to spend with Kelly."

"Turns out she's busy tomorrow."

"That's right, she has a thing."

"A thing. Right. I'm free to help you find the guy."

"That's okay. I really don't need your help."

"It's no problem. That's part of why I came."

"Let me rephrase that. I don't want your help."

"Oh. Sorry. I missed some signals there." He stood. "Gotcha. See you in the morning." He went through the same door Kelly had used.

Good job, Mac, she thought. As she went back out to the patio, she heard a man and woman talking in the kitchen. Aaron and Kelly.

Rather than go straight back to her cabin, Mac went to her van and climbed in through the side door. She and the jukebox stared at each other. "What are we doing here?" The jukebox answered with a quiet hum. Mac slid in a quarter and was not at all surprised when lights and the sounds of "Silent Night" filled the space. She *was* surprised by the vision showing her sitting across the aisle from J.B. on what she recognized as one of Oklahoma City's light rail cars. She was wearing the nice outfit she'd brought with her. Her hair was up in a way she rarely wore it.

MAC FOLLOWED the smell of bacon to the dining room. She expected to find Aaron and Kelly sharing whispers and giggles, but the room was empty except for steaming food warmers and three place settings. Her phone said it was precisely seven o'clock. Before she could worry about what to do next, Aaron and Kelly came in through different doors. Aaron used the one Mac had come in and Kelly came through the door to the kitchen. She was talking to someone through the door as it closed. "Thanks again, Kimi. Enjoy your days off. You'll need the energy. We've got a bunch of executives coming in for a retreat." She made air quotes as she said 'retreat,' and then turned to Mac and Aaron. "Well, dig in. I promise this will be the best breakfast you'll have all day."

"You should put that in the brochure," Aaron replied as he lifted a cover and used his hand to waft bacon and sausage scents toward his face.

"Sleep well?" Kelly asked Mac.

"Great. Thank you. And thanks again for putting me up and feeding me. Dinner was awesome and breakfast smells like it will be just as good."

"It will be. You know, except for the fruit at dinner and the condiments, everything for both meals traveled less than ten miles to get to my kitchen. One of the benefits of being in Oklahoma City."

Aaron's plate and mouth were already full when Mac hesitated with a fork in her hand. "Sorry for being so curt last night. I can't explain why, but I feel like I need to solve the jukebox mystery on my own."

"No apology necessary. You're the boss. I was wrong to press you."

"What did I miss?" Kelly interjected. "You were on a roll when I left. Should I have stuck around to keep you headed in the right direction?"

"It's all good," Aaron said. "We just had a miscommunication about the jukebox Mac's trying to sell."

"I'm not sure if I'm selling it. I'm just looking into its history."

"What's special about it?"

Mac told how she discovered it in the diner and its unique Christmas theme. She recounted her efforts to find anything about it online. Finally, and with some apprehension, she told about finally locating a jukebox expert in Oklahoma City.

While Kelly processed the story, Aaron jumped in. "There's more to it than that, isn't there?"

Mac tried to appear calm. "What do you mean?"

He addressed Kelly. "I talked to the previous owners. It was a strange conversation. They talked about the jukebox as if it was a person instead of a machine. 'They're meant for each other,' I think he said." The room fell silent except for the sound of Aaron chewing and swallowing his next bite. Then he said, "And then there's the lights and music."

∼

A STEW OF EMBARRASSMENT, anger, and, surprisingly, relief flipped Mac's stomach and colored her face. "What do you mean? Jukeboxes are supposed to play music and flash pretty lights." She dared Aaron to go farther.

He did. "No jukebox plays music so perfectly or shines so brightly as your Christmas Jukebox. I've heard systems housing a dozen speakers and costing over a thousand dollars that sound like a transistor radio in comparison."

"And you know this… how? Have you been spying on me?"

"First, please take a breath. I'm not trying to upset you. I want to help. Second, I was not spying on you but was coincidentally in the right place at the right time." He continued before Mac's moving lips formed any words. "Last week at the shop, I went out the back way, remember? Well, I returned to ask what time you wanted me back but heard you talking so I didn't open the door. I thought you were on the phone. Then I heard the music and saw lights under the door. And then last night I saw lights in the trees and looked out the window.

They were coming through the windshield of your van. I also heard Christmas music."

Kelly, who hadn't moved since the conversation started, said, "I heard the music, too. Thought it was coming from a passing car or carried on the wind from the neighbors."

Aaron said, "There's something special about that jukebox. If you still feel like you have to solve its mysteries by yourself, I'll head back home today. I just wanted you to know I'm willing to help without wondering about your sanity." He tested a smile and got a relieved smile in return.

"If I told you the whole story, you would question more than my sanity. Heck, I question my own sanity." She looked up from the table and into Aaron's kind eyes. "But I could use the help. Just trust me to share what I can when I think I should, okay?"

"Deal."

"Let's go get some coffee."

CHAPTER 11

On the way into town, Mac told Aaron about her encounter with J.B. at the Starbucks and expressed her concern that she had left a poor first impression. Aaron's next question dashed any hopes she had that he would just go along without digging into the story.

"You know his name and what he looks like but nothing else?" he asked as they got out of the van.

"I don't actually know his name. I just got tired of calling him the guy from the jukebox and shortened it to J.B."

"How did you recognize him when you saw him yesterday?"

"I saw a picture. No more questions. Remember our deal."

"Sorry. So, what's the plan? Wait for him in the coffee shop?"

"That's what I was thinking earlier, but you can help me do it better and avoid another awkward encounter. He's never seen you before, I hope, so you can wait in the shop." She held up her phone. "I'll go across the street and watch people come and go. When I see him, I'll text you."

"Then what?"

"Then, I guess you see where he goes. He must live or work around here. If we find out where he ends up for the day, we might be able to get a name and contact info."

"Why not just walk up to him and ask him if he owns an antique shop and knows a lot about jukeboxes?"

"That sounded like a question."

"Fair enough." He pointed up the sidewalk. "I'll just go get a coffee I don't need and can't afford."

Mac crossed half the street but had to wait for a train to go by before going on to the CVS. Aaron had already disappeared by the time she found a good wall to lean against. If the store weren't right between two train stations, she could have sat on a bench, pretending to wait for a train. She could tell, though, that neither stop had a clear view of the Starbucks. Her phone vibrated. "All set."

"Me too."

Foot traffic was busier than last time, and Mac lost confidence that she could examine every single face. She texted Aaron to remind him what J.B. looked like just in case he made it past her. As she looked up from her phone and shifted her focus to the sidewalk across the street, she saw him. He wore the same sort of casual business clothes and carried a leather messenger bag that she must have missed the day before. He was two storefronts away from the Starbucks when she texted, "Coming."

Aaron replied with a thumbs-up emoji. Mac could see into the crowded coffee shop and hoped that Aaron had situated himself well. She held her breath as J.B. slowed in front of the Starbucks and looked at his watch. He looked at the door, shook his head slightly, and then kept moving at a brisker pace than before.

Mac's fingers danced across her phone. "Didn't stop. Follow?"

"Me or you?"

"Both!" She had to wait until a couple with a stroller walked past before she could join the stream of pedestrians. Trees and traffic blocked her view of the other sidewalk except for brief glimpses. J.B. was gone. "See him?"

"Nope."

Frustrated, Mac continued to scan faces as she followed a strolling family that was in less of a hurry than she was. She was thinking of crossing the street when lights flashed, warning traffic that a train was coming. She recalled the last vision and called Aaron. "Try the train stop. Maybe that's why he's rushing."

"Okay. Hold on, I won't hang up."

Mac could hear Aaron's breath and the occasional "Pardon me." As a train passed her, Mac saw the stream of pedestrians parting as Aaron rushed to the corner where he could cross to the train stop. *He's not going to make it. I hope that's not J.B.'s train.* But it was. Mac's view of the train stop cleared, revealing J.B. waiting expectantly behind the yellow line on the platform. As the train slowed, Aaron appeared but stopped short and turned around. He caught sight of Mac and threw up his hands as he said, "I don't have a ticket!" He tried to turn back toward the ticketing machines but commuters trying to catch this particular train pressed against him. Mac heard someone say, "Dude. You're making us miss this car. Here. Think ahead next time, okay?" Suddenly, he just popped through onto the platform and joined the group as it hurried forward and onto the train.

"Aaron? Aaron! Do you see him? Is he on the train?" The call ended.

～

"Better to text. Sitting right behind him, I think."

"Pic?"

"Not now. No view. Try l8r."

"K"

The next few minutes seemed like hours. She didn't look up from her phone but resisted the urge to ask for an update. Finally, a picture appeared in her conversation with Aaron along with a text. "This him?"

The image, taken through the train window, showed J.B. in profile as he walked past. Mac was sure it was an accident, but Aaron's photo was sharp and composed as if for an ad in GQ. "Definitely!"

Her phone rang again. "Hey," she answered.

"Hey. We're at the end of the line. He's walking toward an office complex and I'll try to see which building he goes into. I think he noticed me eyeballing him on the train, so I don't want to get too close."

"Thank you, Aaron."

"I could still just approach him and ask him about the jukebox, if you want."

"I don't." Her answer had more of an edge than she intended. Softer, she added, "Not yet, but thanks."

"You're welcome. Okay, he's going into a courtyard shared by four buildings. Hold on… 924. And the street is… 10th. He's at 924 10th street."

"Awesome. Now we have something to go on. Even if I can't figure out where he works…"

"He works at his shop, right? Isn't that what we're looking for? Shouldn't be too hard."

"Right," Mac stammered. "But he might not have been going there. At least we have another clue, another place to look for him."

"Now you sound like a straight-up stalker." Aaron laughed.

"You did the stalking. I stayed in one place. You followed him across town." Mac smiled at the phone.

"Speaking of which… you'll need to come and get me. I don't have any cash and don't want to buy a pass just to get back downtown."

"You could always beg at the machine like before."

"Funny. I'll get my cardboard sign."

∽

SHE'D NEVER SEEN Aaron with his hands in his pockets, but there he was, hands shoved deep and face neutral, almost sad. He was leaning back against a telephone pole and had to pull his hands free to generate forward momentum when he saw the van. She would have considered the new look on his face as one of victory if she hadn't just seen the expression it replaced. His smile now seemed counterfeit. He got in and pointed at a group of buildings with his thumb. "He's in one of those buildings. I hope you don't mind, but I asked Nicole to poke around online and see if any of the tenants have anything to do with antiques or collectibles."

"I don't mind at all. Great idea, in fact." She pulled into traffic. "And thanks again."

"You're welcome. Now what?"

"I guess we wait to see what Nicole comes up with."

"We could also get the lay of the land. Check out the shops and ask around about jukeboxes and experts."

"I've been in most of the big ones several times, but never looking for jukeboxes. We could also visit the smaller shops. There are a couple good thrift stores in the area, too. Even if we don't learn anything about J.B., I might find a few things to flip and pay for this trip."

They spent the day driving from shop to shop. Mac enjoyed being reminded just how much she loved the hunt. She was also glad to have something useful to distract her while Aaron asked questions, and she created answers. She spent several hundred dollars she didn't have on items she hoped would at least double her money.

At four-thirty, Aaron said, "Why don't we go back to the Starbucks in case J.B. stops on his way home? It would give you another chance to approach him about the jukebox."

"Actually, I was thinking about getting a hotel and catching up with him on the train in the morning." She replayed the latest vision in her head. "We'd have a few minutes to chat and he might be more likely to visit with a fellow passenger than someone who walks up to him on the street or in a coffee shop."

He answered with a less-than-enthusiastic "Okay." After a few seconds of silence, he turned and added, "I'm good for one more day." His expression told Mac not to argue. She also didn't argue when he arranged for another night at Kelly's.

∼

THE CHRISTMAS JUKEBOX

KELLY WAS STRETCHED out in a patio lounger when Mac and Aaron got back to the ranch. Her eyes were shut against the sinking sun, and Mac wondered if she was asleep. "How'd it go?" Kelly said, her eyes still closed.

"Okay," Mac answered.

Kelly sat up and swung her long legs over the side of the chair so she could face Mac and Aaron. "Mystery solved?"

"Not quite," Aaron said. "We found the guy but weren't able to talk to him."

"The jukebox guy?"

"The jukebox guy."

Mac interjected, "It's complicated. I literally bumped into him yesterday - spilled coffee all over myself - and was too embarrassed to say anything. Aaron rode the train with him, so we know where he works."

"I thought he worked at his antique store." Kelly got up and led the way into the air conditioning.

"We're not sure if he owns the store, works there, or just consults."

"About jukeboxes." Kelly cocked her head and Mac looked away. Kelly continued, "Seems to me you're going through a lot of trouble to ask a guy about a jukebox. Are you sure that's all it's about?"

Kelly's sly grin and twinkling eyes made heat rush to Mac's cheeks and ears. "Yes, that's it." she stammered.

"Uh, huh. What do you think, Aaron? Is Mac acting like a business woman or a woman woman?"

"Oh, no. You're not dragging me into this whole thing." He waved his hands. "Whatever else is going on, I'm trying to solve a jukebox mystery."

Kelly turned back to Mac. "What's he look like?"

"Who?" Mac immediately regretted playing dumb.

"Who, indeed. Okay, girl. Spill."

Mac looked at Aaron, who had taken a few steps back and was now leaning awkwardly against the bar. He shrugged his shoulders as if to say, 'You're on your own.'

Mac said, "Do you believe in destiny?"

"Like love at first sight? Meant to be together? The one and only?"

"Yeah."

"Mostly. Is that the deal with the jukebox guy?"

Mac chose her words carefully. "Something special happened the first time I saw him. I can't explain it. I just knew we were connected. Or were supposed to be connected."

Kelly held Mac's gaze and continued to nod her head for several seconds after Mac stopped talking. Finally, she said, "The universe likes to steer us sometimes."

"The universe?"

"That's what I call it. Maybe it's God or Karma or something else, I don't know. I believe that, most of the time, we're left to bounce around, finding love and meaning along the way. But every once in a while, the universe needs to nudge things into place to keep the whole thing balanced."

"A week ago, I would be rolling my eyes. But now…"

"Love at first sight. The universe pointing you in the right direction."

"Has it ever happened to you?"

"No. Not at first sight." Kelly looked at Aaron. "Take Aaron, for instance. We met, liked each other, spent time together, and grew pretty close. Then I bumped into someone else and bounced away from Aaron."

Mac asked, "How about you, Aaron? Do you believe in fate or destiny?"

"Not like I used to. I'd rather believe that life is random than that the universe doesn't like me."

CHAPTER 12

Aaron watched from the back seat as the two most beautiful women he had ever met in person chatted. Kelly was stunning and knew it, not in an arrogant way, but she carried herself as a member of the club. Mac was not as traditionally gorgeous and didn't appear to even want to be in the handsome people club. Her beauty didn't reveal itself fully until she walked and smiled and looked you in the eye.

This morning, though, she was nearly Kelly's equal in the looks department. That wasn't surprising, considering the fact that Kelly had spent the better part of an hour helping her get ready. For a train ride. Aaron was still reeling from the Kelly tsunami that had, in less than forty-eight hours, figuratively and literally swept him into the back seat and her into the driver's seat of Mac's jukebox project. He was now a bystander as Kelly drove her car downtown to deliver Mac to the train stop.

"You'll be fine," Kelly said. "Just plop down right next to him and ask him if he knows anything about jukeboxes. The worst thing that could happen is he thinks you're using a really bad pickup line."

Mac pushed a rebellious lock of hair back behind her ear for the tenth time. "I guess. It's not like I've never spoken to a stranger. But, man, am I nervous."

"Don't worry," Aaron interjected, "guys dream about moments like this. A gorgeous woman walks up and starts a conversation? You'll be making his day."

Mac adjusted the visor's makeup mirror and met his eyes. "Really?"

"Really. Just be Mac."

"Just be back before midnight or my car turns into a pumpkin and Aaron and I turn back into mice," Kelly said as she signaled to pull over. "Out you go. Knock him dead."

"Or... just make a great impression," Aaron corrected. "We'll watch from over there and text you if we see him before you do."

"Thanks," Mac said as she got out and shut the door. She immediately opened it again to release the jacket corner she'd closed it on. Aaron watched her walk away in one of Kelly's skirts worn over navy tights. Her fringed jacket didn't really belong, but it was Mac being Mac and that was okay.

"Our little girl is all grown up and off on her first date," Kelly said as she drove on down the block looking for a place to park.

"This is all just a little bit too weird, don't you think?" Aaron asked.

"Love is weird."

"That's what I mean. She hasn't even formally met this guy, but she's acting like he's The One." He paused as he watched Mac cross to the median. "Sorry, I forgot. The *universe* is in control."

"Do I sense a little jealousy, Mr. Stiles?"

He shook his head. "I've given up on love, remember?"

"Aw, come on. I was jealous when you showed up with her, you know."

"Good." He tapped Kelly on the shoulder and pointed through the windshield. "There he is, coming toward us on this side of the street. Gray blazer, open collar. See him?" Kelly still hadn't answered by the time he finished texting Mac. "Did you see him?" He asked again.

"Not only do I see him, I think I know him."

As the train pulled away, Aaron remembered the picture he had taken to show Mac. He retrieved it and handed his phone up to Kelly.

"That's Jared Brownfield. He's the attorney that helped me untangle the mess that had the ranch tied up for months after Dad died." She handed the phone back and pushed her eyebrows together. "But, unless he's changed careers recently, he doesn't own an antique store."

"Maybe jukeboxes are his hobby," Aaron said half-heartedly.

"This is big, Aaron."

"Big?"

"Big as the universe."

~

Kelly parked in the commuter lot next to the last stop on the light rail line. A few minutes later, Aaron spotted J.B. walking alone toward the office complex. He was about to text Mac when she appeared at the stoplight and waved. Aaron and Kelly looked at each other.

Mac appeared a full inch shorter as she walked to the car and got in. She sat in silence, staring out the windshield.

"So?" Kelly said.

"So, nothing. I lost my nerve."

Aaron shifted in his seat so he could see Mac's face in the mirror. Her eyes were glistening, but she wasn't yet crying. "But you saw him," Aaron stated.

"I saw him. He saw me. We smiled at each other. Then I just froze. It was just like what I saw in the…" she stopped suddenly, took a breath, and finished, "… just like I imagined. Right up until I couldn't go up to him."

"It's okay, Mac," Kelly said. "You'll get him next time."

"There's not going to be a next time. This has all been silly. I'm heading home as soon as you get me back to my van."

"No, you're not. You are going to meet Jared Brownfield."

"Who?"

"Jared Brownfield. The guy you've been following for the past two days."

"You know him?"

"The universe and I both know him."

∽

"Can I ride in back?" Mac asked through Aaron's open window. Kelly was pumping gas and Mac had just returned from the convenience store with a diet soda, a Mountain Dew, and three homemade brownies that, according to Kelly, were out of this world.

"Sure." Aaron got out, sheepishly took the green bottle, and climbed in the front seat. "Do you have enough space back there?"

"Yes. Thanks. You can even come back a little if you need to." The smalltalk was a welcome break from the conversation they had been having. Not to mention what Mac was about to reveal.

After Kelly got back in the car and everyone had devoured the brownies that lived up to their reputation, Mac adjusted her position so that neither Aaron nor Kelly could see her eyes in a mirror. She took a breath and opened her mouth to speak, but Kelly beat her to it. "You know what the odds are that I know the man you think you're supposed to be with?"

"It would be a pretty big coincidence," Mac offered.

"It's no coincidence. I can feel it. Whatever you want to call it - let's stick with the universe for now - something is driving you two together."

"Coincidences do happen, you know," Aaron offered.

"True. But let's review what we know. Correct me if I get anything wrong, Mac." Kelly punctuated each point by tapping the steering wheel. "You buy a mysterious jukebox from an elderly couple who don't offer any information about it. You feel compelled to learn about the machine, so you start researching. You run into someone who gives you a lead about a shop somewhere that might know something about a Christmas jukebox. Did I get that right?"

"Pretty much." Mac didn't know if Kelly was making what she about to do next easier or harder.

"That's pretty thin," Aaron said.

"Impossibly thin," Kelly said with some irritation. "That's my point.

Internet searches led to coffee shops which led to Oklahoma City which led to an impossibly coincidental meeting with a guy Mac recognized from, what, a thumbnail image on Facebook?"

"Something like that," Mac answered.

"And this guy starts the bells ringing and birds singing just by being polite when you bump into him."

"Uh, huh."

"That's no coincidence. That's the universe. And that's all before you got involved, Aaron, which led to me, which led to Jared and the chance for Mac to close the circle."

Mac pressed herself even further back in her seat. "I believe you're right. But there's more to it." She closed her eyes but could feel Aaron and Kelly straining to catch a glimpse. "Even if you believe everything you just said, you might think what I'm about to tell you is crazy. That maybe I'm crazy."

"Try us," Kelly said evenly.

"The jukebox showed me Jared."

"What?" Aaron asked.

"The lights you saw? They are like a projector showing me things from the past and, I assume, the future." She let the story spill out of her. "I put a quarter in and music plays, but not like any other jukebox or stereo system. It's almost playing in my head. Then images appear, life-sized and right in front of the jukebox. They move like a hologram or something, but the only sound is the music. Then they stop and the jukebox goes back to normal." Mac opened her eyes to see Kelly and Aaron staring straight ahead out the windshield. She waited for Kelly to pull over and politely ask the delusional person in the back seat to get out of her car.

When Kelly spoke, her tone was matter-of-fact and conversational. She might have been asking how the brownie tasted or if Mac thought it was going to rain. "How long do these visions last? How many have you had?"

"They last as long as whatever song it's playing. I've seen eight, but I don't think there are many more left."

"Why do you say that?"

"There's a counter that clicks down after every one. It started at twelve, I think, but now it's at four."

"Can I see it? The jukebox, I mean?"

"Sure." Now Mac was beginning to wonder about Kelly's sanity.

Aaron said, "This is a lot to take in."

"Tell me about it," Mac replied.

"And in these visions, you and Jared are together?" Aaron asked.

"In a couple of them, yes. What else could it mean, anyway? I saw me first, and then him, and then us."

Kelly said, "I believe you, Mac. This is the Universe's way of directing some bouncing balls. Like the flippers on a cosmic pinball machine. We just need to make sure you win the game before running out of chances."

They rode the last few miles in silence as everyone processed what Mac had just revealed. As Kelly pulled up behind the van, she said, "It's in there, huh?"

"Come on, I'll show you." They walked over and Mac opened the double doors revealing the jukebox, which was now surrounded by the other items she'd picked up during the day.

"How do you plug it in?" Aaron was looking around for an outlet or extension cord.

"It doesn't always need electricity."

Kelly climbed in and pushed a small side table out of the way. She squatted across from the jukebox and ran her hands up its sides, finally resting them on top. "Can I try it?"

Mac handed her a quarter, which Kelly dropped into the slot. The sound of it landing in the coin box echoed around the van, but nothing else happened. Mac looked at Aaron and said, "It only works for me, I guess. If we plug it in, it will probably play like a regular jukebox."

Kelly got out, shut the doors, and brushed her hands off on her jeans. "Right. Well. I have a call to make. With any luck, you'll be meeting Mr. Jared, 'Jukebox' Brownfield this evening." She put one arm around Aaron's waist, the other around Mac's, and guided them into the house.

CHAPTER 13

"It doesn't have to be a total lie, Mac," Kelly said.

"But I don't plan to open any new shops. I'm not sure I can keep the one I have."

"If your business really took off, and you had more money than you knew what to do with, would you think about expanding?"

"I guess."

"Does Oklahoma City seem like a good place for an antique and collectible gallery?"

"Sure. There are plenty here already."

"So we aren't lying, we're just being optimistic and forward-thinking."

"I don't know, Kelly. It just seems wrong to start a relationship with a lie."

"Fib. It's a fib. I guess you could just tell him the truth and see what happens. 'Hi, I'm Mac and my magical Christmas jukebox sent me to find you so we can be together forever.'"

"Fine. We'll go with the fib… for now."

Kelly was helping Mac pick out another one of Kelly's outfits. The two women could have been twins when it came to size, shape, and taste in clothes. "Business casual should work. I'd love to put you in this little number, but it screams, 'Look at me! I want to date you!'" She put the short black dress back in her massive closet and pulled out another outfit. "We have a winner."

An hour later, Kelly and Mac said goodbye to Aaron as he relaxed on the patio. "I'm not sure who he was staring at, but at least one of us must look really good," Kelly whispered as they walked to her car. Without thinking, Mac turned to look at Aaron. He was still looking their way and gave her sheepish wave.

Kelly didn't even bother trying to find a parking place. She pulled up in front of the restaurant, let the valet open their doors for them, and gave him the keys.

She and Mac were dressed like a couple of professionals catching a bite after work. Kelly wore creased black slacks and a billowy pink blouse. Mac wore the same navy skirt as she had on the train, but with a white blouse under a jacket that matched the skirt. She'd allowed Kelly to curl her hair and apply more makeup than Mac had worn since high school. She drew the line at high heels, though, and wore a simple pair of black flats.

"I think I might throw up."

"Nonsense." Kelly didn't break stride and Mac felt magnetically attached to her side as they strode through the restaurant. Two men at the bar gave them a long look, but Kelly didn't seem to notice. She was focused on a man at a table near the back.

Mac was focused on the woman sitting across from him.

"Jared?" Kelly leaned forward and flashed a smile that Mac was sure had served her very well over the years.

"Kelly. Great to see you." Jared stood and shook her hand.

"Same here. And thank you so much for letting us crash your dinner for a second." She glanced at Mac and then turned back to Jared. "It's amazing how things line up perfectly sometimes, isn't it?"

"I'd love to catch up sometime, Kelly, and see how that ranch of yours is doing. Give me a call when we both have more time."

"Sure. Love to. We won't hold you much longer. This is Mac, the friend I told you about on the phone. She's leaving town in the morning but mentioned this afternoon that she's looking for a lawyer." Kelly turned her smile up to eleven. "And I told her I knew the man for her."

"Nice to meet you, Mac. What kind of representation do you need?"

Mac hoped her memorized answer didn't sound memorized. "I own an antiques gallery in Sloan, and I'm thinking of expanding to Oklahoma City. I need a lawyer who knows the local system. Texas and Oklahoma might be next to each other but, apparently, they do things quite differently."

"That's for sure," said the woman Mac had been trying not to stare at.

"Sorry, this is Andrea, one of my colleagues." Jared gestured and everyone nodded and smiled. He added, "Actually, this sort of thing is more up her alley than mine." He reached out to Andrea, who was already pulling a business card from her purse.

"I'd be happy to help," she said as Jared passed along her card. "Call me next week and we can talk about the details."

Jared shifted from one foot to the other, and Andrea glanced down at her appetizer. Kelly said, "Well, thanks again, Jared. Mac, we'd better get going before they figure out how to bill us for the consultation." Her smile and the hand she put on Jared's arm defused any offense he may have taken.

"Good to see you, Kelly, have a good night." He said goodbye to Mac with a nod. Andrea said goodbye with a wave.

As they waited for an elderly couple to make their way out the door, Mac stole a glance over her shoulder. Jared and Andrea were leaning toward each other. Jared was talking and Andrea was laughing.

∽

∽

THE BUSINESS CARD was simple and elegant. Mac ran a finger across the raised print. Under the firm's name was a phone number. Andrea's name and areas of expertise were printed on the back of the card. After staring at it for a minute while she mentally rehearsed what she would say, she dialed.

"Hello," said a female voice.

Mac hesitated, waiting for the rest of the standard receptionist welcome, but it didn't come. "Hello. May I speak to Jared Brownfield, please."

Another pause. "Who's calling?"

"This is Mac Talley. I'm a potential client."

"Mac. Are you the Mac who came by the restaurant last night?"

"Yes, that's me." Realization drained the color from her face.

"This is Andrea. You called my direct number. But you're looking for Jared?"

"That's right. I, umm, Kelly suggested, umm, I have something to discuss with him." Mac completed the fifth lap of her office.

"If it's about relocating, I'm still happy to help."

"It's about something else, if that's okay."

"Sure. Hold on, let me see if he's available."

Mac second-guessed everything she had just said except for 'Hello.'

"Hello? Ms. Talley?"

Ms. Talley. "Hi. Yeah, this is Mac Talley. From last night at the restaurant."

"Sure. I remember. What can I do for you?"

Most of what she had prepared abandoned Mac. "Well, I, umm, see, this is awkward. I could have found an attorney on my own, but Kelly recommended you so highly that I felt you were the one. I'm sure Andrea is great but, if you are available, I would prefer to work with you."

"As I said, Andrea does this sort of work all the time and is, quite frankly, better at it. I'm the firm's estate planning and management expert. But… I suppose I could review your expected needs and either represent you…" His tone changed slightly. "… or convince you to engage Andrea."

"Thank you so much. When can we meet?"

"A phone call is probably sufficient, but I have a client waiting for me right now. How about..." Mac heard keys clicking "... tomorrow at nine-fifteen?"

"Tomorrow's perfect," Mac lied. "In fact, I'm going to be in town anyway and can just pop over to your office. I won't take a minute longer than a phone call, I promise." Two more lies.

Jared took a few seconds too long to respond. "Okay. I'll see you tomorrow. You have the address. We're on the third floor right across from the elevator."

"Great. Thanks again."

"Goodbye, Mac."

"'Bye."

A surge of hope, excitement, and anticipation pushed out the doubt and worry she'd been feeling since the night before. *Maybe the universe and I are back in sync.*

~

MAC CONSIDERED her safe arrival at Jared's office as more evidence of divine intervention in her quest. Three hours of fitful sleep should not have been enough rest to safely drive the two hundred miles. Part of the trip was a drowsy blur. She was wide awake now, though, as she checked her hair and makeup in the rear-view mirror. She wasn't dressed up like she was at the restaurant. She wore her nicest jeans, a plain blouse, cowboy boots, and her fringed jacket; the one from the vision. Her hair was pulled back in a ponytail which she tugged and snugged against the hair tie as she walked to the office building.

"Can I help you?" A very young man - an intern, Mac guessed - asked as she got off the elevator.

"Yes. I'm here to see Jared Brownfield." She noticed motion at the edge of her vision and turned her head just enough to see Andrea look out through the glass door of her office. Mac spun the other way, hoping that she looked different enough that Andrea wouldn't recognize her.

"Is he expecting you?"

"We have an appointment scheduled for 9:15," Mac answered.

The intern mashed a button on his desk phone. "Mr. Brownfield, a Ms…"

"Talley. Mac Talley."

"… Mac Talley is here for a 9:15." He gave Mac a practiced smile while he listened to Jared. "Go on back, Ma'am. Third office on your right."

She said, "Thank you" but wanted to say, *"Don't call me Ma'am."* She didn't look Andrea's direction but felt her gaze.

Jared was waiting for her in the hallway. He greeted her and ushered her through the door, waiting until she sat in one of the fake antique armchairs before settling into the other. When he crossed one leg over the other, the tip of his sensible dress shoe was inches away from Mac's shin. She was glad that denim hides goosebumps. He took a legal pad from the corner of his desk and withdrew an expensive pen from the pocket of his jacket. "I don't want to be crass, but you do need to know that we will bill you for any actionable advice I give you today."

"Oh. Of course."

"You plan to expand your Texas-based business into Oklahoma. Is that correct?"

"Yes." Mac folded her hands in her lap to hide their shaking.

"Is it a corporation or a sole-proprietorship?"

"Corporation. LLC? Does that sound right? I'm sorry, but my former partner handled most of the legal stuff."

"So, you may need help with more than just interstate business issues?"

Mac swallowed hard. "Yes and no. Yes, there's more, but no, I don't really need help with interstate business issues."

"I don't follow." Jared uncrossed his legs and straightened.

"It's a little embarrassing but, please, hear me out." She gave him a moment to respond, but he didn't. "I saw you on the train the other day and - I can't believe I'm doing this - I thought you were… are… attractive. My friend Kelly was with me. And she recognized you. When I told her about the good-looking guy on the train, she told me she could introduce me."

THE CHRISTMAS JUKEBOX

Jared said, "Uh, huh," so quietly that Mac could barely hear him over the rushing sound of her own heartbeat.

"You know the rest. The story about my business got a little out of hand. I'm not looking to expand any time soon. I just wanted an excuse to meet you."

"In my world, we call that fraud," he said flatly. Mac's eyes were still widening when his serious expression eased into a comfortable smile. "Relax. I'm kidding. Actually, I'm flattered, but I'm afraid your - and Kelly's - production was for nothing. I'm… off the market."

"Wife? Girlfriend?"

"Neither. Just not looking right now."

"I understand. But…" Mac's mind superimposed J.B. from the visions over the man she was talking to. "…don't you think it's more than a coincidence that you, me, and Kelly were all in the same place at the same time? I mean, I don't even live here, and Kelly hardly ever comes to this part of town. Couldn't it be…"

"Fate? Are you suggesting that we were somehow *supposed* to meet?"

"Yes. I do."

"Okay, Ms. Talley. Again, I'm flattered by the attention, but I need to get back to work." Jared stood and gestured toward the door.

A half dozen responses tumbled into Mac's mind, but she couldn't untangle them in time. A meek, "Sorry to bother you," was all she could manage. She imagined that everyone in the office knew what just happened and was watching her take the walk of shame to the elevator. She didn't have to imagine Andrea. They made eye contact and shared a look that communicated an hour's worth of conversation in an instant of woman's intuition.

CHAPTER 14

A woman she'd never seen before was behind the front desk of the Starcrest Ranch. "Checking in?"

"No. I'm actually looking for Kelly. Is she around?"

"I think she's in the kitchen with Kimi."

Apparently, knowing how to get to the kitchen was the desk clerk's way of testing how well Mac knew Kelly. Mac said, "Thanks. I'll find her," and headed through the dining room. Kelly and Kimi were having an animated conversation, so Mac knocked on the door.

"Who's knocking on my kitchen door?"

"It's me, Mac."

"Come on back." Kimi waved as Mac worked herself into a corner where she hoped she would be out of the way. Kelly said, "Sorry about the curt greeting. Usually, anybody who belongs in the kitchen just comes in and employees who shouldn't be here know to stay away. Only a guest would knock and fussing at them reminds them not to wander around. Then it gives me a chance for one of my award-winning apologies."

"Does it work?"

"I guess. Nobody's ever come back here twice, and nobody's ever checked out early because the owner is mean." Something Kimi was doing distracted Kelly. "Hold on a sec', Mac." After a whispered conversation with her chef, she walked back to where Mac was standing. "What brings you to Starcrest?"

"I went to see Jared this morning."

"Step into my office."

Kelly's 'office' was a pantry full of all the dry ingredients for whatever Kimi made for the guests. Kelly sat on a stack of boxes and gestured to another stack for her friend. Mac said, "It was horrible. As soon as he knew I wasn't looking for a lawyer, he basically threw me out."

"That doesn't sound like him. And why did you tell him? I mean, what did you tell him?"

"I said it wasn't coincidence that we saw each other and that you knew him and could introduce us. I told him I thought he was attractive and wanted to meet him."

"What did he say when he 'threw you out'?"

"That he wasn't interested and that I should leave." Kelly scowled so Mac added, "He was polite about it, but his message was very clear."

"I hate to say it like this but look at it from his perspective. Not only does he not have a client, he has a potential stalker."

Kelly's words hit Mac like a sack of flour. "But it's the universe at work, right?"

"You know that, and I know that, but he doesn't. Not yet."

"Yet." She sighed. "I messed up, didn't I?"

"Yep."

"I should have talked to you first."

"Yep." Kelly popped the p.

"Now what?"

Kelly looked at her watch. "Now, I go see how many things have gone wrong at the front desk and try to fix them before my new clerk quits. You go home and nurse your wounds while the universe figures out how to get things back on track."

As Mac threw her arms around Kelly, she marveled at how close she'd come to this remarkable woman in such a short time. No wonder Aaron fell in love with her.

∽

The sign in the gallery's door was turned to 'closed' and the place was dark. The door did not respond to Mac's tugging, which meant that Nicole must have closed up shop at exactly 6:00pm, if not a few minutes before. Her key was already in the lock when she changed her mind and started to walk the familiar path to the workshop. Her stride was stiff at first but loosened up as her knees and legs got used to a position other than the right angles they'd been in for the past couple of hours. She was glad to be wearing her jacket; the local weather had finally noticed that Christmas was just around the corner. The most direct route to the shop took her away from the main streets and through a couple of industrial alleys. This section often made her nervous after dusk but, tonight, she didn't mind the solitude and lack of traffic.

She let herself into the workshop and flicked the light switch. The last pair of tubes finished blinking to life just as she settled into her recliner. "You sure are making this hard, aren't you?" Mac wouldn't have been surprised if the jukebox had answered, but it just sat there. She fished in her pockets for a quarter but couldn't find one. "Figures," she said as she looked around the room for likely sources of change. She shoved each hand into the gap next to the recliner's seat cushion. "What are the odds?"

The dull, dusty quarter she rescued from the chair looked like it could have fallen from the pocket of the first person to fall asleep in the recliner. "Okay, Christmas jukebox, time to redeem yourself." She slid the quarter into its slot and watched the machine choose a record and get ready to play. "Baby, It's Cold Outside" echoed around the room in all its tinny glory, but there were no extra lights. There was no vision. There were no answers.

∽

Rather than go back the way she came, Mac decided to join the group of walkers and shoppers that kept the downtown area busy and in business. It had been weeks since she'd been on this end of the street in the evening. The last time was with Richard for dinner. At the thought of dinner, her stomach reminded her that she hadn't eaten anything since a gas-station bag of Frito's. She walked past Richard's favorite place and into a restaurant she had never been to but with a name that was somehow familiar. It was larger than it looked from the outside, with a bar on one side and a dozen or so tables on the other. Strings of white lights draped from hooks in the ceiling along with holly and mistletoe. Mariah Carey sang "All I Want for Christmas" in the background.

The hostess was coming back to her station from deep in the restaurant. She gestured with a menu for Mac to go to the table she was clearing. "How many?"

"One. Just me."

"Your server will be with you shortly."

Mac closed her eyes and took in the sounds of Christmas and the smells of a dozen peoples' favorite foods. Something moved nearby. When she opened her eyes, she was looking at a smiling Aaron. He said, "It's about time. I didn't think you were ever going to check out my other job."

"I'm not. I mean, I didn't know this was where you work. I just stopped in for dinner."

"Really? That's quite a coincidence."

"That's all I'm getting these days, apparently. Not that any of them are working out for me."

Aaron looked at her thoughtfully for a few seconds and then caught the eye of the bartender by tapping his wrist where a watch would be if he wore one. Then he held up five fingers. The bartender frowned and nodded.

"What's up?" Aaron sat down across from Mac.

"I went to see Jared this morning."

"Refresh my memory. Who's Jared?" He grinned and Mac couldn't help but smile in return.

"The guy who is clearly not on board with *the universe's* program." She put air quotes around 'the universe'.

"I take it the visit didn't go like you hoped."

"Not even close." Mac described her visit with Jared and followed up with an account of her conversation with Kelly. "Do you think she's right?" Mac asked. "Am I a stalker?"

"Nah. You're at least two steps away from a stalker." Aaron looked at the bartender who was giving him the wrist tapping gesture. "Seriously. Don't worry about it. I'm not as big a believer in fate as Kelly is but, if it's supposed to happen, it will happen, right?"

"I guess."

"Look, I've got to go. My shift ends at midnight. If you want to talk after that, call me."

Mac smiled. "Or I could just wait eight more hours and see you at the gallery."

"Or you could do that."

As she walked back to her van, she used her phone to look up Jared Brownfield online. She found a number that was one digit different than Andrea's. She dialed it and hoped he wouldn't answer. He didn't.

"Hey, Jared, this is Mac Talley. I just wanted to apologize for my awkward visit this morning. Have a good night."

She'd hoped for closure but felt the opposite. This wasn't over.

∽

MAC IGNORED the call because she didn't recognize the number. In fact, she often let people she did know go straight to voicemail, especially if they were asking about money. Nicole was pretty good about staying ahead of the bills that could shut them down, but a couple of suppliers and craftsmen were anxious to get paid. The business still had room on its line of credit, but trying to bring in more money than they spent seemed to add fifty pounds to Mac's karmic weight. She smiled at the thought of 'karmic weight' because that particular phrase would have never come to mind before she met Kelly. Or the jukebox.

The phone buzzed again and, this time, the caller left a message.

THE CHRISTMAS JUKEBOX

Mac didn't even listen to the whole thing. She called back immediately. "Hey, sorry I didn't pick up. Didn't recognize your number."

"No problem. I'm calling from the front desk. I have news." Kelly's voice had a playful air of mystery about it.

"Spill." Mac stopped pacing and sat down.

"It turns out that our friend Jared is somewhere between the depression and acceptance stages of grief. The girl he was about to propose to pulled a Kelly and walked away."

"'Pulled a Kelly?'" Mac knew what it meant but was curious to hear her explain it.

"You know what I mean. It's what people like me and what's-his-name do when we're afraid to commit."

"Richard."

"Yeah, Richard. Anyway, it hurt Jared bad. Not only won't he date, he's dialed back most of his relationships with women."

"And he told you all this? You must have been closer than you let on."

"No and no, we weren't. He didn't tell me."

"Huh?"

"Andrea did." Kelly let that sink in for a few seconds. "We had a real heart-to-heart. She became a friend and confidant when Jared was in love with the girl of his dreams. When it fell apart, Andrea tried to console him, but he pulled away. She thinks he was afraid she was trying to slide in on the rebound, but I doubt it. For a guy *that* in love, the whole universe turns upside down when the road to bliss ends at a cliff. He threw up walls and is only now starting to let his closest friends in. Andrea's still on the outside, probably because she's an available woman."

"And she told you all this?"

"I have a gift. What can I say."

Mac started thinking out loud. "So maybe the universe, or whatever, is using the jukebox to help me bust through his wall. Maybe I'm supposed to be the real girl of his dreams."

"Maybe. But I'll tell you what. It doesn't sound like he's anywhere near ready to get back on the cosmic merry-go-round. Ease off for a while and see what happens."

"Okay. I understand. Thanks, Kelly."

"That's apparently what I'm here for. To help other women find love while I torture as many men as possible."

"I don't believe that for a minute. There's someone out there for you. I'm sure of it."

"From your lips to God's - or the Universe's - ear."

CHAPTER 15

Aaron tried to keep his eyes on Mac while he gave her an update about the items he had been restoring. Instead of an elephant in the room, he thought, they were avoiding a weird Christmas jukebox.

Mac asked, "Are the end table and the Uncle Sam bank are ready to go?"

"Not quite. Sammy could use some paint if you want him to look like new, but that's beyond me. He's clean and functional, though."

"We'll get about the same amount for it, regardless. People are funny. Real collectors won't even make an offer if the restoration isn't perfect. They'd rather take it as-is. Beginners or nostalgia shoppers will pay more if it looks like new or like they remembered it. Same item, completely different perspectives."

"The table had been painted, and not by a professional. I could tell from the underside that it was solid cherry, so I stripped and sanded it."

"It looks awesome."

He felt more pride than he expected. "Thanks. I was afraid that it might be a rare antique, but then realized that I couldn't do any more damage than the guy who slathered it with Rustoleum."

Mac closed her eyes as if retrieving something from memory. "I paid, like, two hundred for both pieces. We'll get up to four hundred for the bank and another couple hundred for the table, easy. I can live with that."

"It's good to see you smile. Seems like you've been really stressed the past couple of days."

"It has been rough." She jabbed a finger toward the jukebox. "That thing is going to be the death of me."

"I hope not. If you die, what will I do for a day job?" While Mac chuckled, he added, "It's even better to hear you laugh."

"Don't get used to it." She strained to hold back a grin. "We still have a lot to look at."

Aaron showed her the pieces he had either started working on or evaluated. Mac's approval seemed genuine and flowed freely. By the time they were finished, Aaron felt an inch taller. The tour ended where it began, near the jukebox. He rested a hand on it and asked, "What about this? I know it's special to you and that you don't want me to work on it too much, but should I clean up the outside at least?" He paused while Mac stared dumbly at the machine. "Do you think you'll ever sell it?"

"Lately, I spend more time wishing I'd never bought it." She sat in the recliner while Aaron leaned against a concrete pillar. "Thanks for being so diplomatic, by the way."

"Diplomatic?"

"You aren't too hard to read, Aaron. I watched you while I told about the visions that came along with the lights and music you heard. You don't quite believe me, do you?"

Good job avoiding the elephant, Aaron. "I believe that you believe."

"Okay."

A surprisingly comfortable silence embraced the three of them. Mac stared at the jukebox, Aaron stared at Mac, and the jukebox made the barely perceptible humming noise that said it was plugged in. Although nothing changed about the lighting and nothing moved in the room, a silvery glint caught Aaron's eye. The edge of a quarter peeked out from underneath the jukebox. He bent down, picked it up, and, with a feeling he could not identify, slid it into the jukebox's coin slot.

The sleigh and carousel of records began to move, just as he had watched them do before. The needle settled onto the platter and "Do You Hear What I Hear?" started to play. Mac eased forward in her seat. Tears formed in her eyes as the light inside the jukebox became too bright to look at. Streams ran down her cheeks as the sound seemed to move from the speakers directly into Aaron's head. Their eyes locked for an eternal split second before they both watched Jared and Mac move around a room decorated for Christmas. They and a perfect tree were in focus, but the rest of the room and the several other people moving around the edges were blurry. As the song came to an end, Jared and Mac looked at each other, their faces stretched with joy.

"You can close your mouth now," Mac said as the counter changed to three and the room fell silent.

"I, umm, owe you an apology. A couple, actually."

"No. The fact that I'm not alone anymore makes up for everything."

"What does it mean, do you think?"

"It means I can't give up. I can't not be that happy again."

Aaron set his jaw and asked, "What can I do to help?"

∼

THE TIRE under Mac dropped into a pothole. Mac's head thumped into the passenger window. She woke up with a sore neck and a tiny, gravity-defying pool of slobber caught in the divot beneath her lower lip. "Wow. How long have I been out?"

"Half an hour or so." Aaron glanced at the map on his phone. "We'll be downtown in another twenty minutes."

Mac was surprised to have fallen asleep in a vehicle, even though she hadn't slept much the night before. Aaron had replied to her midnight text with an offer to drive so she could focus on how she was going to approach Jared. That moment was now less than an hour away. She rummaged through her purse until she located a travel-size tube of toothpaste. She didn't bother looking for a brush because there wasn't one. Her finger did the job, at least killing the taste and smell of whatever had been awake and growing in her mouth while she was asleep. She pulled down the visor and bobbed around so she could see every part of her head. While she put on a little lipstick, she said, "Thanks again for driving. I probably would have been fine but would have hated every minute."

"No problem." He gave a two-fingered salute. "I serve the jukebox."

Neither of them smiled. Aaron's eyes were open and focused on the road, but he wasn't blinking very often. Mac was glad when the traffic picked up and his head began to swivel as he shifted from highway to city mode. Downtown rose in front of them until an exit ramp and tire-testing cloverleaf dumped them into Oklahoma City. Mac pulled her jacket from the back of her seat and put it on the floor next to her purse. "Just drop me off a block before the Starbucks."

As she shut the door behind her, Aaron returned her friendly smile, but not the wave. He pulled into traffic and disappeared around the next corner. Mac was now in a different kind of traffic, and it took her a few strides to match the flow on the sidewalk. As she approached the coffee shop, she somehow knew she would get there before Jared.

The coffee cup shook in her hand even before she took her first sip. She looked out the window at where Jared would appear if he took the same route as the other two times she had laid in wait for him. She was rehearsing her speech again when he came through the door. He looked as tired as Mac felt. When he stepped aside to help form the coffee queue, he saw Mac. His gaze barely stopped on her, but she knew he'd seen her. He bought his coffee and walked out without looking her way again.

"Wait. Please." She had to take three steps to each of his two.

Jared did not respond. He sipped his coffee and pretended to watch where he was going, as if this weren't the thousandth time he'd made the trip.

Mac gave him some space but stayed close enough that she was sure he could hear what she was about to say. "Kelly told me to put myself in your shoes. This girl shows up out of nowhere and comes on to you like a groupie with a backstage pass. You have every right to be wary and even a little scared." He appeared to fight a glance her way. She continued, "I just ask you to put yourself in my shoes for a minute."

Jared jaywalked, crossing the road at an angle to reach the train stop. Mac stayed with him, earning a couple of horn honks. The train pulled in at the same time, and Aaron boarded without breaking stride. Mac had to jostle against other passengers, managing to make it aboard just as the doors closed. Jared had found a seat surrounded by people, even though the back half of the car was almost empty. Mac stood right in front of him. She put one hand on her hip and the other through a strap hanging from the ceiling. "Look at it from my perspective." She peered down at the bridge of his nose as he stared straight ahead. "You see a picture of someone and just know... really *know* that you're supposed to meet."

Everyone but Jared was now looking at Mac, but she kept her eyes locked on him. "What do you do? You can't sleep. You can't deny that something weird is going on. You have to find the person you saw, don't you?"

As a dozen eyes shifted from Mac to Jared, he got up, took Mac by the free arm, and waited for her to free her hand from the strap. He led her back to a pair of seats facing each other. "Look," he said. "I deal with my share of odd people in my profession and I don't read you as completely crazy."

"Thank you?"

"Still. We can pretend to see things through each other's eyes all we want, but the fact of the matter is that you don't know me. I don't know you. Even if 'fate' led you to me, I don't have to play. I'm not going to play. My life is where I want it right now and I'm sorry yours isn't." The train slowed at the next stop. "Good luck and goodbye. Seriously."

Mac stayed seated as he got off the train and turned around to wait for the next one. She road to his stop at the end of the line, got off, and crossed to the other side to catch the train back to where she started. When Jared got off the next train, they had a final conversation with their eyes. Mac tried to convey that she was sane. It didn't take much effort to know what Jared was saying. Stay away.

CHAPTER 16

"Can you cover the Anderson closing for me?" Jared stood in the doorway of Andrea's office.

"Sure. What's up?"

"It's my only appointment this afternoon and I need to do something. Thanks."

He left before his colleague could put on her friend hat. He went back to his desk, where he continued to ignore the day's emails and voice messages. The cursor blinked in the search window, enticing him to type her name. He finally did. 'Mackenzie Talley Sloan Antiques'

The few pictures that came up confirmed that the woman he'd met was, indeed, named Mac who actually ran a gallery. The 'About Us' photo on their website showed Mac with her partner Richard Polson. They looked like more than business partners.

He closed the browser window and opened his firm's contact application. Thirty minutes later, he was pulling up in front of the Starcrest Ranch.

"Jared? Ouch!" Kelly caught her hip on the corner of the reception desk as she rushed around it.

111

"Are you okay?"

"Yeah. I need to either have that corner rounded or start wearing padding." She rubbed her side. "I do that at least once a week."

He reached out for a handshake, but Kelly ignored it and gave him a friendly hug. She asked, "That was quick."

"What was quick?"

"It's only been a couple days since you said we should catch up." Before Jared could shift his mental gears, she added, "At the restaurant. You wanted to see the ranch."

"Sure." He followed her into a corner of the lobby and eased into a leather club chair across from a fireplace. Kelly sat on the raised hearth. "It's great," he said, "I mean, I'm sure it's great. But that's not why I'm here."

"Really?" Kelly's curiosity almost looked genuine.

"Really. It's about your friend Mac."

"Uh, huh."

"You're not going to make this easy, are you?"

Kelly cocked her head and flashed a heart-stopping smile. "I could say, 'Make *what* easy' but I'm feeling nice today." She leaned forward and put a hand on the arm of his chair. "I take it that Mac called you again."

"No, she showed up at the coffee shop this morning and followed me."

"This morning?"

He looked at his watch. "About five hours ago. 'Awkward' does not adequately describe our conversation."

"This morning. What did she say?"

This girl should be a litigator. "Pretty much what she told me the other day in my office. But, this time, she mentioned you." Kelly didn't blink and her smile barely faded. "She said you told her to put herself in my shoes."

"That's right. I also told her to give you some space." Her eyes joined the smiling party. "But love is a powerful force."

Jared shifted back in his chair so quickly that it slid an inch on the rough wood floor. Kelly took her arm from the chair so her hand could join its companion in her lap. Jared said, "I will be the first to admit that I don't understand women. Never have. In fact, I'm not sure any male has ever fully comprehended any female. But I do believe that you need more than a picture and a name to love someone."

"Eventually. But I meant exactly what I said. Love is a powerful force, just like gravity. You don't need to know where something is going to land or how it's going to bounce to know that it's heavy. Mac saw you and was drawn to you by emotional gravity."

"Love."

"Love," Kelly echoed.

"At first sight."

"Never happened to you?"

"Not like that."

"Look, Jared, I don't know what to tell you. Mac and I met less than a week ago, but I know people. She is honest, sincere, and trying to make sense of events and feelings that most people never get the chance to encounter."

"She's stalking me, Kelly."

She hardened instantly. "So get a restraining order."

"I will if I have to."

"Close your eyes."

"What?"

"Close your eyes, Jared." He did. "Now picture Mackenzie Talley the last time you saw her."

"Okay..."

"Now imagine her with a gun and a knife and screaming 'If I can't have you, nobody will.'"

He opened his eyes, embarrassed, and looked back at Kelly. Her face was soft and open again. "I get your point. But I don't need that kind of drama in my life right now."

Kelly waited a long minute as if deciding whether to allow whatever sentence was forming in her mind to escape her lips. She finally asked, "Did she mention anything about a jukebox?"

"What? No."

"Hmm." She stood and reached for his hand. He took it and let her pull him out of the deep chair. As he struggled to get upright, he realized that he could have easily pushed himself out with both hands. Kelly was making it harder, not easier. He wanted to scowl, but that smile of hers made him just shake his head. Kelly said, "Mac's a good soul. She's just new to the way the universe works." She didn't release his hand. "Come on. Since you're here, you might as well see what you helped me rescue."

∽

"No," Kelly said.

"But…"

"No, Mac, it's just not a good idea."

"What about fate? The universe?"

"I told you not to rush. Now, you'll be lucky if he doesn't call the cops."

"Seriously?"

"No, I talked him off the ledge yesterday." While Mac was still trying to put words to her surprised reaction, Kelly continued, "He came by to chew me out for putting you two together."

"Sorry about that. Was he actually going to call the police?"

"I suggested it, in fact. That's how I forced him to think it all the way through. He left here satisfied that you are harmless and that you won't bother him anymore."

"How am I supposed to make the visions come true if I don't 'bother' him?"

"Maybe the visions show something farther in the future. Or maybe it's a possible future that depends on him. I don't know. I'm just pretty sure - no, I'm darn near certain - that nothing will get him to talk to you again."

Mac looked at Aaron, who was listening over the speakerphone. She said, "The jukebox showed us another vision."

"Us? Who's us?"

"Mac and me," answered Aaron.

"You saw one?"

"It's just like she described. Like nothing I've ever seen."

"What was it about?"

Mac answered. "It showed me and Jared together at Christmas. This Christmas."

"And that counter above the coin slot?" Aaron added, "It's now at three. We think that means time's running out."

The line was quiet for so long that Mac asked, "Are you still there?"

"I'm here, but I don't know what else we can do."

"Ask him to come here to the gallery. Tell him I have something to show him that will explain everything. If he'll come and listen to me, I'll leave him alone forever if that's what he wants."

"You're going to show him the jukebox."

"Uh, huh. If the universe wants so badly to get us together, it can show him what it showed me."

"It *sounds* like a good plan, but you didn't see him. He is in a bad place and not just because you're stalking him."

"I'm not stalking him."

"Chill, Mac, I'm kidding. But look at it from his perspective."

"Will you try?"

After a long pause and an audible sigh, Kelly answered, "I'll try."

∼

KELLY STARED AT HER PHONE, wondering how she got herself involved with Mac's drama and why it was so hard to get out. Getting out was her specialty, just ask Aaron. She slid the phone back in the pocket of her jeans and went back to work replacing a hinge on the main house's big front door. A persistent squeak had survived several attacks with oil and WD-40. It was time to stop trying to make the ancient hinge behave and start new. She tightened the last long screw and tested the door. The new hinge worked silently and flawlessly, but something was still not quite right. "Seriously?" Kelly moved the door back and forth, listening to the screech of the other hinge. Now, she was going to have to deal with the slightly quieter member of the front door duet. With a sigh, she wiped her hands on a rag and went to get the oil. But her mind was not on the door project. It was turning the Mac project back and forth. It squeaked, too.

Her phone was now on the table in front of her between a can of 3-in-one oil and the WD-40. She had to make the call, but she wasn't doing it for Mac or Jared. She simply knew that she had to do it. Destiny depended on her. She didn't know what she would say, but she had to do her part, whatever that turned out to be. She picked up the phone, found Jared's number, and dialed.

"Hello?"

"Hi, Jared, this is Kelly."

"Hi, Kelly." He sounded pleasant but reserved.

She panicked as, for the first time since 3rd grade, she was at an embarrassing loss for words. She looked around her empty lobby as if someone might appear to rescue her. A sudden calm came over her, restoring her confidence. "You're probably wondering why I called."

"I am a little curious, yes."

"Honestly, I'm not sure. I just had an overwhelming urge to call and say hello."

"So, this isn't about your friend?"

"I don't think so," Kelly heard herself say.

"You don't think so." He sighed so loudly that it sounded like he blew into his phone. "This has been the strangest couple of days I can remember."

"Me, too. What if we just pretend that I'm following up on your visit to the ranch. We had a nice visit, but I forgot to thank you for all your help getting the estate squared away and the business started."

"But you did thank me. In fact, you thanked me so much that I was able to buy a new BMW."

Kelly laughed without adding the extra spice that made men want to hear it again. She hoped Jared's own laughter hid the slight snort at the end of her chuckle. They talked about her plans for the ranch. They reminisced about her parents, who Jared had known before they passed away. They talked about their plans for Christmas. They even talked about the weather. They did not talk about Mac.

After she hung up, Kelly was confused and tried to make herself feel guilty about not furthering the universe's plans for Mac and Jared. But it all felt so right. She knew her conversation went the way it was supposed to go. She suspected that Mac wouldn't see it that way.

CHAPTER 17

"She wouldn't say, but I think she has Jared with her," Mac said to Aaron and Nicole.

"When will they be here?" Nicole stopped refolding the vintage scarves that curious but unserious shoppers had rummaged through.

"She is about half an hour away, headed straight for the shop. Nicole, do you mind closing up?"

"I was hoping to see one of those visions you guys keep talking about. It's my turn, don't you think?"

"I can do it, Mac. I don't mind," Aaron answered.

Mac put a hand on Nicole's shoulder. "It is your turn. But I don't want to jinx it. The jukebox waited a long time before letting Aaron see a vision, but now we know it will. I can't risk having a new person there who might keep it from showing one to Jared."

"I get it. Maybe next time."

"Definitely."

Aaron followed Mac out the door. She asked, "Do you mind driving? That's your car out front, right?"

"Sure. I knew there was some reason I got a good parking space for once."

Mac checked her phone ten times during the five-minute drive.

THE CHRISTMAS JUKEBOX

She was out of the car almost before it was completely stopped. By the time Aaron parked, locked the doors, and walked around the car, Mac was already inside the shop. "Grab a couple chairs from that dining set," she said. They placed two chairs on each side of the recliner, forming a semi-circle facing the jukebox. "I hope this works," Mac said.

"Yeah," Aaron answered.

A noise made them both turn. Someone was trying to open the door, which had latched behind Aaron. He rushed over and opened it. Mac made sure the front of her blouse was tucked in properly and tried to look casual.

Kelly exchanged a few words with Aaron as she came through the door. He closed it without looking out or hesitating. Kelly said, "You don't look happy to see me."

"I am. I just thought - hoped - you might have someone with you."

"Sorry, Mac. Really, I am. I called and was ready to invite him, but it didn't feel right. He's not ready."

Mac gestured for Kelly to come to the jukebox. "Come look at this." She pointed at the counter above the coin slot. "Three songs left, four if it plays one after it hits zero. Every song is about Christmas. Every vision has included Christmas. Three songs, three weeks until Christmas. He doesn't have a lot of time to get ready."

"I understand. And I believe that you've been seeing what fate has in store for you and Jared. There was simply nothing I could do." She held up a quarter that she must have been carrying when she came in the shop. "Can I?"

"Go ahead."

Kelly slowly, almost reverently, inserted the quarter. When it hit the bottom, the jukebox came to life. Three faces almost touched as they peered into the machine and watched the mechanisms go through their motions. After the first few seconds of "Here We Come A-Caroling", Mac stepped back and settled into her recliner. Kelly turned and asked, "No vision?"

"No. I thought it might show you like it did Aaron. I don't know why it didn't."

"I think I do," Kelly replied.

"Why?" Aaron asked.

"Because it didn't need to." Kelly shifted her gaze from Mac to Aaron and back again. "Seeing a vision would have been spectacular, but it wouldn't have made me any more certain. I believe you. I believe in fate."

"At this point, the person without proof might have more faith than either of us," Mac answered while nodding toward Aaron.

"I believe everything is going to work out like it's supposed to," Kelly answered.

∽

"You guys go ahead. I'm not hungry." Mac returned the last chair to its place under the dining table as Aaron and Kelly headed for the door.

"You're sure?" They asked in unison.

"I need to think. Some alone time while I'm not driving might help me process what's going on."

Aaron ushered Kelly out the door by placing a hand on her lower back. Mac involuntarily recalled the touch of Richard doing the same. She missed him or, at least, the thought of him. A confidant. A friend. Why couldn't she just take a break from relationships like Jared did? Richard had been gone for just a few weeks and yet Mac was already lonely.

The recliner was empty and alone again; the jukebox's companion and co-conspirator. Mac sat down and stared at the humming machine for a long minute. "What do you want from me?" she said, her voice bouncing around the shop. "What am I supposed to do now?"

The jukebox responded by putting the carousel into motion. It rotated until a record settled onto the turntable. The first bars of a familiar Christmas song began to play. Before Mac could put a name to the tune, the record skipped, jumping back to the beginning. A brilliant white light flooded the guts of the jukebox until it burst out in a beam that filled the space in front of Mac. The five seconds of scratchy music played, popped, and played again. Mac's eyes adjusted to the whiteness as an image formed within the beam. The jukebox projected a vision of itself sitting where Mac first saw it. What she could see of the diner was empty and mostly dark. The jukebox glowed and the strings of Christmas lights twinkled.

The light and vision ended abruptly. The only sounds in the shop were Mac's anxious breathing and the whirring of the machine as it returned the record to its proper place. Then the counter moved from three to two.

Mac's shoulders began to heave as a month's worth of stress collected at her throat and eyes. She sobbed for no particular reason but a hundred collected ones. Everything she had seen and everything she had done seemed to be for nothing. Even the jukebox knew it was time to give up. She had failed. Richard was gone before she had a chance to understand why. Jared was gone before she had a chance to know him at all.

She cried until the worst of the anger, sadness, regret, and self-pity was captured in a soggy McDonald's napkin. Then she tossed her second-favorite curse at the jukebox and went home.

∽

MAC WAITED while Nicole looked over her shoulder at the door she'd just come through. Her keys were still in her hand, even though she hadn't needed them to unlock the gallery. Mac greeted her with a cheery, "Good Morning!"

"Morning." Nicole's reply sounded more like a question.

"Coffee's still hot. There's a cup on your desk."

"Thanks, Mac. What brings you in so early this morning?"

"I work here." She hoped her smile conveyed the joke.

"I mean, have you solved the mystery of Jared and the Christmas jukebox?"

"Not sure there's a case to crack anymore, honestly. Nothing I did seemed to work. In fact, everything I did made things worse. It's like when Richard left. Time to accept fate and move on."

"What happened?"

Mac had hoped to get more than one minute into the day before talking about the jukebox. She changed the subject. "I don't want to get into it right now. What I'd like to do is unravel the biggest mess Richard left us with."

"You mean the online auction thing?"

"That's right. We either owe a bunch of listing fees or they owe us a couple thousand dollars in sales."

"Actually, both."

Mac stared while Nicole looked from her to the floor. "Both? You figured it out?"

"Yes and no. The listing fees don't line up exactly with the final sales. That's what confused us."

"And?"

Nicole hesitated. "And I found Richard and asked him about it. He explained how it worked and who to talk to. It's all good now."

Mac didn't hear anything after the word 'Richard.' "You talked to Richard?"

"Emailed, actually. I searched some more online and found out that he's…"

Mac cut her off. "I don't want to know." All the emotions that she had purged the night before returned, filling her from the vee in her throat to the top of her head. "How could you do that without talking to me first? Do you think this is still his business? Are you afraid I'm running it into the ground?"

"No. You're doing the best you can. And…"

"The best that I can. That's great. Thanks for the vote of confidence."

"I tried to tell you, but you've not been around. Was I supposed to just text you? 'Hey, Mac, I found Richard. Okay if I ask about the online auction?'"

"That would have been better than getting his help behind my back." Mac cursed for the second time in twelve hours. "He must love the idea of me flailing around. Oh, I can imagine how happy he was to help."

Nicole, who had been shrinking back toward the door, straightened and stepped forward. "Actually, he *was* happy and very helpful. He asked how you were doing and said we could ask him any other questions that come up."

"Here's a question you can ask him:" Mac tried to stop speaking. She knew the next words would light a fire she might never be able to extinguish. Her emotions won. "Where can I find an office manager who won't go behind my back?"

It was worse than Mac had feared. The corners of Nicole's mouth turned down and began to quiver. She raised a shaking, accusing finger. "You don't get to talk to me like that. I have busted my butt for you. Not for Richard or for this 'business' but for *you*." She opened the door, paused, and turned back to Mac. "Maybe during your search for a new office manager, you'll realize that I didn't go behind your back. I *had* your back while you chased your jukebox visions." The gentle tinkling of the bells attached to the door hurt Mac's ears more than if Nicole had slammed it.

∼

"I can only stay until five, and that's if I go straight from here to the restaurant," Aaron said as he hung his jacket on a wicker coat rack inside the door.

"That's fine. I'm just glad you were able to come in on such short notice. I know you were supposed to be off today."

"Where's Nicole? Is she okay?"

"I'm sure she's okay. She needed the day off. I would have covered myself, but I have some errands to run and some suppliers to reassure."

Aaron pressed, "Did Nicole say what's wrong? She was fine when we closed up yesterday. We even had plans to move a few items from the shop to the gallery." He paused as he tried to read Mac's expression. "I suppose we can do that tomorrow, though."

"She might not be here tomorrow, either. She overstepped."

"How?" Aaron leaned against Nicole's desk facing Mac, who took a step back.

"We argued. No, we fought. I found out that she reached out to Richard for help without asking me first. She accused me of neglecting the business and I said she didn't trust me as the boss."

"I'm surprised she didn't tell you, but it wasn't a huge deal. Richard was happy to point her in the right direction."

"You knew, too?!"

"We were together when he texted her back. It was a quick exchange."

"And you think it's okay to ask for help from the guy who abandoned his - our - business?"

"Don't *you* think you're overreacting a little bit? Nicole was just trying to keep things running while you..."

"While I chased visions, right?" Mac had spent all her heat on Nicole. All she had for Aaron was coldness.

"That's not what I was about to say but, yes, I suspect that Nicole worried about you. She doesn't have as much of the picture as Kelly and I."

"So, you both think I'm being unreasonable. Maybe I am. But you know what? I'm the one he abandoned in every meaningful way, so I'm entitled to hold a grudge."

"You don't have to forgive him to get over him, Mac. Can't you see what you're doing to yourself? Open your eyes. If you would look around and see what you have in your life - right now - you might not need a magical jukebox to tell you what to do."

"Thanks for coming in, Aaron, but I think I can manage by myself."

"I hope you're right. I really do."

The bell on the door jingled again, as if counting down Mac's friends. Three, two, one...

CHAPTER 18

With no one around to talk her out of sulking, Mac spent the next hour rattling around the gallery rearranging, updating prices, and freshening the window display. A shadow fell across the manakin as she placed a new necklace around its neck. An older but well-dressed woman was examining the jewelry and other new items. Mac met her as she came through the door. "Good morning. Can I help you find something in particular?"

The woman stretched to see around Mac. "Is Nicole around?"

"No, Ma'am. She's off today. I'm Mac, the owner, and am glad to help you."

"Oh, dear, I'm sorry. I hope I didn't offend you. Goodness, did I have that backward. I thought this was Nicole's place. I saw you in here once before but just assumed you worked for her."

"Well," Mac said as warmly as she could fake, "we all do everything we can to make customers feel welcome."

"That's nice. And good business. My Lamont and I ran a laundry and dry-cleaning business for almost fifty years. Our best customers became more like friends than accounts receivable."

"We feel the same way, Ma'am."

"Doris, please."

"Can I show you something in particular, Doris?"

"No, I really stopped in to say hello to Nicole. I walk past here nearly every day and enjoy starting out with a nice chat with a pleasant girl." She dipped her head and lowered her voice. "Plus, she lets me see any new items before she puts them out on the floor." Remembering who she was talking to, she straightened and put a hand to her mouth. "Oh, my, I hope I haven't just gotten her into trouble."

"Of course not," Mac said while looking at the door. "No trouble at all."

Doris followed Mac's gaze and began to turn toward the exit. "Say hello for me, will you?"

"Will do. Thanks for coming in and have a great day."

The bell announced the departure of one of Nicole's customers. Mac rummaged through an end-table at the front of the gallery. She taped a pre-printed "Please Come Back Tomorrow" sign to the door right below the one she had just turned to read "Closed."

Her disappointment at having to close the gallery for the afternoon deepened when she realized that it probably wouldn't make any difference to the bottom line. Even if Aaron had stayed, the gallery wasn't likely to make much more than what it would take to cover his pay.

By the time she got home after talking to people who wanted money from her, she wondered if she wouldn't be better off just closing the gallery altogether. The thought shocked her because just a few weeks ago, the business was one of the two things that made her happy. One of the two things that defined her.

∼

SHE WASN'T SURPRISED, but Mac was a little disappointed when the gallery was dark and locked when she arrived the next morning. Nicole wasn't there and didn't come in late. Mac couldn't blame her. She didn't even know if Aaron's absence meant anything because she didn't know his schedule. Nicole managed it.

Determined to keep the business running as close to normal as possible, she turned on her computer so she could access the shared calendar to see what needed to be done. After three unsuccessful attempts at logging in, she remembered that Nicole had suggested that they change passwords to prevent "hacking." Nicole had watched a television show that scared her into being more security conscious. Unfortunately, the password Mac chose was so secure that she could not remember it.

She looked at the phone, knowing that the easiest way to get in would be to call Nicole and ask for the password. That would require talking to Nicole, though, and she wasn't ready to do that just yet. Hoping that Nicole had not yet completely mastered computer security, Mac explored her work area. She'd noticed Nicole using a Post-it note to build the impossible-to-remember passwords. Maybe it was still on her desk.

The desk that initially looked as cluttered as Mac's turned out to be covered with a carefully arranged set of piles. The first one was a stack of invoices sorted by date. Next to it was a stack of receipts for items Mac had bought since Richard left. There was a notebook Nicole used to record whatever Mac asked her to do when calling from the road, along with the answers to whatever questions she asked. Already weakened by the evidence of Nicole's commitment, Mac's grip on the resentment she was trying to hold gave way completely when she opened the next notebook. Across the front, in Nicole's unique mixture of cursive and block lettering, were the words, "How Can I Help?"

Mac had only leafed through the first few pages before she started to feel as if she were reading a diary instead of a work document. She closed it after scanning a page titled "Recovering from Richard." After putting everything back exactly as it was, she pulled open the makeshift desk's center drawer and found the Post-it.

She logged into her computer, prioritized her day, and spent it doing the too-many things she should have taken care of rather than dumping them on her friend. Between phone calls, inventory, and making walk-in customers happy, she composed four emails but left them, unsent, in the draft folder. After closing the gallery, she sat back down at the computer and made certain that each email conveyed what she felt as closely as possible.

The day's final task was supposed to be the most cathartic. She created an elaborate entry for the gallery's website. It offered a one-of-a-kind collectible vintage Christmas-themed jukebox. After nearly an hour of work, she paused with her mouse pointer over the "submit" button. At the last second, she shook her head and clicked "cancel."

∼

"CLOSED UNTIL FURTHER NOTICE."

Mac stood on the sidewalk and examined the sign in the front door. Of all the feelings churning within her, two took turns being the most powerful. They had taken turns keeping her awake most of the night. These two emotions would keep her focused and moving through whatever was to come. Like two sides of a record, despair and resolve didn't seem to belong together until played back-to-back.

When she took a step back to make sure the sign was centered, she bumped into someone who had come up behind her. "Excuse me," she said as she turned around.

"Yeah. Watch where you're going. You might step on my toes."

Mac and Nicole looked at each other in silence. Mac said, "I'm so sorry."

Nicole opened her arms wide. "Come here, you." As they embraced, Nicole added, "That was the sweetest, rawest - is that a word? - most wonderful email I ever got."

"I meant every word. I am such a knucklehead."

Nicole let Mac go and pointed at the sign. "What's that all about?"

"I need to take care of something so I'm closing the store."

"Nonsense. We can take care of things for you."

"We?"

Aaron appeared at her other side. "We." He gave her a friendly half hug. "I do have to say that I've received better emails, but yours was in the top 10%."

Nicole opened the door and ripped the sign out of the window. "You won't be needing this."

Mac and Aaron followed her inside. Aaron asked, "Where are you headed… if you don't mind me asking."

Mac winced at Aaron's tentative delivery. "Not at all." She looked from Aaron to Nicole and back. "I spent the night trying to decide whether fate let me down or vice versa. This morning, I decided that it doesn't matter. The jukebox did what it was supposed to do, and I did what I did. It's time to move on. I'm taking it home."

"Need company?"

"No, Aaron. Thank you, but I feel like I have to do this alone. End this… interesting… experience the way it started: me, the van, the road, and a Christmas jukebox. You can help me load it up, though, if you don't mind."

∾

AT ABOUT THE same time that Aaron and Mac each closed one of the double doors on the van, Kelly and Jared each opened and read an email from Mackenzie Talley. Kelly nodded and smiled. Jared deleted it, undeleted it, and spent a few minutes contemplating the rush hour traffic as it moved beneath his apartment window.

CHAPTER 19

Mac arrived at the diner just after noon. The empty parking lot didn't surprise her since the owners' voice mail message said it was closed while they looked for buyers. She pulled up in front so she could see through the windows. Glowing strings of Christmas bulbs provided the only light in the empty building. She was encouraged to see that the furniture and Christmas decorations were still in place. She got out and walked to the door, straining to make out the small letters filling the small sign on the door. The sign echoed the words of the phone message but included a number to call in case of emergency. Mac tried to hold on to the inexplicable certainty she'd felt about being able to bring the jukebox home as she dialed it. She hoped she wasn't calling Happy Gables, Florida. The bleating in her ear that told her the other end was ringing was soon joined by the first dozen notes of "Jingle Bells" coming from across the parking lot. She turned to see Stan approaching from next door.

He looked right at her, answered his phone, and said, "Hello. Is this Mac?"

"Umm, yes, I'm right here." She waved.

"I'm calling to ask if you'd like to join me and Moira for lunch."

"But I called you."

"Did you really?"

Mac hesitated, thrown off guard by the oddly pleasant man. "Yes," she said as she recovered. "I did."

"Well, I supposed *we'll* have to have lunch with *you*, then." He ended the call as he approached the van. He fiddled with his phone for a second and then raised a finger when Mac started to speak. "Moira, Mac's here for lunch."

"I didn't come for lunch," Mac stammered.

"Sure, you did." Stan unlocked the front door and led Mac inside. He pointed to a booth as he walked past it to a bank of switches on the back wall. The diner came to life as the overhead lights, air conditioning, and quiet Christmas music came on. Mac heard the rear door open and close just before Moira appeared behind the counter. She was wearing a green apron with "Stan's Diner" stenciled on it in red.

"Hello, dear. I'm afraid our menu is limited, but the burger and fries are still delicious."

"Sounds great to us," Stan answered. Moira disappeared again, and Stan slid into the other side of the booth to face Mac. "Here about the jukebox?"

"Yes," Mac began, but the diplomatic speech she'd prepared didn't feel right anymore. She couldn't just tell these wonderful people that she regretted buying the jukebox and would like her money back. The single word hung in the air as Stan looked at her patiently and without any apparent discomfort or anticipation.

Moira rescued Mac by coming from the kitchen and sitting next to her husband. "I hope you aren't starving. It takes a few minutes for the grill and fryer to get going."

"You don't have to go to all that trouble for me. I just…"

"She's here about the jukebox," Stan said with a knowing smile.

"Of course she is," Moira adopted the same expression.

"Why do I get the idea you aren't surprised to see me."

"We've been expecting you, actually," Stan answered. "In fact, you took longer than I thought you would. Cost me twenty bucks."

"Don't bring up that silly bet. I never agreed to it," Moira retorted.

She turned to Mac. "I believed you would get quite far along before reaching out for answers."

"I could sure use some. The jukebox you sold me has turned my life inside out."

Stan and Moira shared a look. Stan said, "Told you so."

"Told her what?"

"He told me you were the one who was supposed to get the jukebox. Not that it took me long to agree."

"So, you knew about it? What it does?"

"Why don't you tell us what it did for you," Stan answered.

"It hasn't done anything *for* me. It has done quite a bit *to* me."

The couple sat silently, clearly willing to wait as long as it took for Mac to finish answering. She continued, "I assume you know it has special powers - for lack of a better word. It projected moving images - we called them visions - of people and places in the past and future."

Stan leaned forward. "We?"

"My friends and I."

"You all saw the visions?"

"No, but they believe me." She recalled the vision Aaron saw. "Actually, one other person saw a short vision."

"Just one, though," Moira said.

"Yes. But it was such a relief not to be the only one."

Moira put her hand on Mac's. "I know. It makes one question one's sanity, doesn't it?"

"I thought I was having a breakdown. But the visions were so real, and the counter is counting down. That can't be my imagination."

"What does it say now, the counter. How many are left?" Stan asked.

"Two."

"Maybe you should have come a little earlier," Stan said.

Moira squeezed Mac's hand as she gave Stan a sharp look. "You are not losing your mind. The jukebox really does have special powers. We're proof."

"What do you mean you're proof?"

"That wonderful machine brought us together," Moira said.

"Except I was you, and Moira was whoever you saw in the visions."

"Why didn't you tell me?"

"Two reasons," Stan answered. "First, you would have politely refused to buy the jukebox and run from the diner as fast as you could. Second, the jukebox wants each owner to see for himself - or herself." He smiled apologetically.

"How do you know what it wants?"

"Partly through experience and partly from the previous owner. I found him after the eighth or ninth time the jukebox showed me Moira. He asked a lot of questions and finally confirmed the way it works."

Moira spoke up. "I will tell you this, though. You mustn't assume that your experience will be exactly like ours."

"Moira!" Stan paled. "Don't jinx it. You're awfully close to the line."

"I won't say any more."

"I don't understand," Mac said.

"Neither do we, Stan said. But we trust the jukebox or whoever is using it to bring joy into the world. We don't want to tell you anything that might change what's supposed to happen."

"Trust it, dear," Moira added. "And please tell us how it all turns out."

∽

MAC TRIED to replay every vision as she drove back towards home. Some details had begun to slip away, and she cursed herself for not bringing her journal with her. The most recent vision was the easiest to recall and yet troubled her the most. The jukebox had been alone in the diner as if Mac had never owned it. She had assumed that it was telling her she had failed. Her selfishness and narrow focus had caused her to miss too many prompts, to squander too many opportunities. Even fate could not recover from her incompetence. But that's not how she felt now. She believed that, even if she had blocked, ignored, or destroyed several routes to Jared's happiness, at least one path remained. One path *had* to remain.

The drive to Sloan was over before she knew it. Mac turned off the ignition and listened to the engine tick as it cooled in the afternoon shade of her building. She looked in the rearview mirror at the darkening shape that was the jukebox. "What are you trying to tell me?" The answer came not as a voice or a flash of inspiration, but as the merging of all the thoughts and questions she'd been pondering since she left the diner. "You want to be home. You *need* to be home."

She turned the key again, checked the gas gauge, and pointed the van back toward Stan's Diner.

~

THE DINER WAS JUST as it was when she'd first arrived half a day ago, only darker. The Christmas lights filled the room with hundreds of fuzzy shadows. Stan and Moria's house was dark. Even the porch light was out. Mac put her ear to the door and thought she heard a television or radio. She was was poised to knock when she thought better of it and pulled out her phone.

"Hello?"

"Um, Hi, this is Mac."

"Hello, Mac, did you forget something?"

"Yes. But not something I left. Something I should have left. Look, I know it's late and I'm really sorry to bother you but…"

"No problem. How can we help?"

"Can we talk again… in person?"

"Tonight?"

"If possible."

"Sure. When will you be back?"

"I'm outside now. I didn't want to just bang on your door."

Mac could hear shuffling movement over the phone and saw a light come on in a back window. Stan said, "We'll be right there."

Two minutes later, Stan and Moira appeared at the door wearing matching flannel pajamas. Stan's wiry gray hair stuck out like he was auditioning for the part of Doc in a Back to the Future sequel. Moira was as put together as when Mac had last seen her. They both wore coats over their pajamas and gardening shoes on their sockless feet.

"Hi," said Mac, sheepishly.

"Great to see you again," Moira answered.

"And so soon!" Stan added with a wink.

Mac gestured toward the van and diner. "Can we go inside?"

Stan shook the keys he was holding. "I figured we'd need these."

Once they were settled in a booth, Mac told them again about the last vision and what she thought it meant. Stan and Moira listened silently, nodding occasionally. When she finished, Stan said, "So you want to leave it here."

"If you'll let me." She paused before he could say the 'of course' that she knew this wonderful and kind man would offer. "But there's more to it than that. I think the only way the jukebox is going to be able to do whatever it's trying to do is if I bring people here. I think it's giving me one more chance on its home court."

"Dear, we've been waiting a lot of years for the chance to repay the debt we owe the jukebox and whoever or whatever controls it," Moira said, "Of course you can use the diner - and us - however you see fit." She put her hand on Mac's.

"We'll even cook dinner," Stan added, "And give you a group discount on the tab."

Moira shook her head and squeezed Mac's hand. "Just ignore the old man with the wild hair. You just tell us what you need and when you need it."

"You got a hand truck, or should I get mine?" Stan got up and went to the door.

"It's already strapped to one."

"Let's get 'er inside, then." He grinned and held the door open for Mac.

After they rolled the jukebox into place and released it from the dolly, Jack reached down to plug it in. "Don't!" Mac almost shouted and then said, much more softly, "I don't want to risk wasting a vision."

"Gotcha. But I wouldn't worry about it. This machine knows what it's doing and will do it whenever it wants to."

"I'm counting on it," Mac said as she looked at the '02' displayed on the counter. "I'm counting on it."

CHAPTER 20

Mac was - mostly - relieved to see that both Aaron and Nicole were at the gallery when she arrived the next morning. She knew they expected this to be the first day of their post-jukebox life. She hoped they could shift that date a week or so into the future. They were rearranging a display cabinet and had their backs to the door when the bell announced Mac's arrival. The unguarded looks of affection on their faces made Mac feel less alone than at any time since she bought the jukebox.

"Did they take it back?" Nicole asked.

"Sorta."

"No refund, huh?" Aaron's smile faded.

"I didn't ask for one. They told me that the jukebox brought them together. They knew what it was, and that I was supposed to be the one to get it next. I just have to see this through." She went on to explain her new interpretation of the last vision and why she left the jukebox with the Caldwells.

"So, you're going to give Jared another chance," Aaron said.

"I'm going to give the jukebox another chance, if it's not too late. I wasted a lot of time trying to make this all about me. No wonder Jared won't talk to me. It's a miracle that you guys haven't bailed, considering how I dragged you into my drama."

"We like a good drama, don't we, Nicole."

"Sure do!"

"If you can live through a few days more, I'd appreciate it if you'd keep the business going while I finish this. I'll cut the store hours if I have to, but we really need the Christmas shoppers' money."

Nicole started to speak, but Aaron put a hand on her arm to silence her. "No, we will not manage the store while you follow the jukebox." Mac and Nicole both stared at him. All three wore serious expressions until Aaron's cracked. "All three of us will work together to keep the store open and help the jukebox do whatever it's trying to do."

"Are you sure? It's my problem."

"Your problems are our problems," Nicole answered.

Mac selected the best two of the dozen words that played across her mind. "Thank you."

∽

MAC FELT the millisecond-long jolt of surprise that sometimes comes when deep thinking about the past gives way to confronting a different present. She had spent hundreds of hours and thousands of miles in the passenger seat while Richard drove. Now, Aaron was doing the driving while she reviewed her updated notes about the visions.

"Your lips are yellow," Aaron said without looking away from the road.

"Huh?" She pulled the visor down and considered herself in the small mirror. Then she looked at the highlighter she'd been using to mark her journal. A yellow ring surrounded the space where the cap met the marker. "That's what I get for using my teeth to pull the cap off." She rummaged around in the console, coming up with a probably-clean napkin.

"Are we about there?" Nicole asked from behind Mac. She was in

THE CHRISTMAS JUKEBOX

the rear-facing jump seat. "It's weird moving backwards and I'm getting a little queasy."

Aaron consulted the navigation app on his phone. "Sixteen more minutes."

Mac spent most of that time trying to get the last splotch of yellow ink off her lip. Finally, she asked, "Nicole, do you have any lipstick I could borrow?"

Nicole dug through her purse and handed a tube over her shoulder. "Here you go. I hope it's your color."

"I'm not sure what my color is these days, but I am sure it isn't yellow."

The lights were on in the diner. Other than the sign on the door, the restaurant looked like it was open for business. Shadows moved deep beyond the window as Stan and Moira made the place ready for their guests.

Nicole lagged behind Mac and Aaron while she took in a few deep breaths of the cool Texas air. "That was too close for comfort. I hope they won't take it personal if I don't eat anything."

"They won't. Plus, I'm sure Aaron will take up the slack."

"Definitely," Aaron agreed as he pushed the door open for Mac and Nicole.

Mac wasn't sure, but it seemed as though some of the Christmas decorations that had been missing the last time she was in the diner were back in place. The jukebox certainly looked at home in its corner. It glowed and hummed contentedly.

Stan didn't even wait for the door to finish closing. "Hi, Mac! Who are your friends?"

"This is Nicole," Mac said as she pointed to a still-pale Nicole. "And this is…"

Aaron joined Mac as she answered. "Aaron."

Mac put her hand on Aaron's arm to prevent another duet. She said, "This is Aaron Stiles. He and Nicole work with me at the gallery."

"Do they know?" Stan asked with raised eyebrows.

"I know. In fact, I've seen one of the visions," Aaron answered.

Stan said, "Pretty neat, huh?"

Moira said, "Nice to meet you, Nicole and Aaron."

"You, too, and yes, the jukebox is amazing. And mysterious," Aaron said.

Nicole, whose face was now only slightly more pink than gray, said, "Pleased to meet you," and headed for the restroom.

"Speaking of amazing," Stan said, "how do you two like working for the Amazing Mac?"

Stan and Moira were both angled toward Aaron as if ready to herd him into a corner. Mac eased in next to Aaron, turning the triangle into a square. "Aaron's the amazing one. He can turn a flea market reject into something I can sell for a good profit." She let Aaron bask in the Caldwells' approval for a few seconds and then added,

Six chairs surrounded two square tables that had been pushed together in the middle of the room. "A booth isn't quite big enough," Stan explained. He added, "Did you say there would be four of you?"

"Maybe," Mac answered. "We invited Kelly, my new friend from Oklahoma City, but we don't know if she's going to make it."

"Let's eat first, then, to give her time to get here if she's coming."

Moira asked, "Any vegetarians or peanut allergies?" Three heads shook. "Good. Burgers all around with fries cooked in peanut oil."

After they ate (and Nicole managed to recover enough to eat some French fries), Aaron said, "That was the best hamburger I've had in a long time. Maybe forever."

"It's the secret seasoning and cheese combo," Stan said. "Don't even ask for it. I'm taking it to the grave."

"Don't listen to him. You can buy it at the supermarket. The only secrets are the fifty-year-old grill and the sixty-five-year-old griller," Moira said.

Mac was focused on her phone. "Kelly can't make it. I'll fill her in later."

Moira took off her apron, draped it over a stool, and joined the group around the tables, sitting around the corner from Stan, who was at the end with his back to the jukebox. He wore a knowing grin that Mac thought bordered on a smirk. Mac sat at the opposite end of the tables. She held up her journal, which had Post-it notes sticking out of all three edges. "I've written down everything I can remember about each vision and marked whatever seems important." She opened to the page marked by the first Post-it. "I thought we would go over them together and see if we can figure out what the jukebox is trying to do. Then we can decide how to help it."

Nicole and Aaron looked around and nodded. Aaron said, "Makes sense to me."

Stan and Moira were smiling but not nodding. Mac asked, "What do you two think?"

Stan said, "Keep going."

She bobbled the notebook, and it fell to the table. She found her place again and said, "Okay. The first vision was of me as a little girl. For a while, I thought that meant the jukebox was trying to do something for me. Now, I believe it was just telling me it knows about me." She looked around the table. "Thoughts?"

"Makes sense to me," Aaron said again.

Mac gave her interpretations of the next couple of visions, which also made sense to Aaron. Nicole suggested that the woman in the third vision may or may not be Mac. When pressed, Mac had to agree, although she *felt* like it was Mac.

As she began to describe the next vision, Stan got up and went to the jukebox. Mac stopped mid-sentence as he took a quarter from his pocket and dropped it in the jukebox.

"What are you doing?! We only have two visions left!"

"What am I doing?" He said with a big grin. "I'm cutting out the middleman."

As the normal workings of the jukebox began to transform into another super-sensory vision, Mac couldn't help but think that it was happy to be home. The perfect sounds of "It's Beginning to Look a Lot Like Christmas", the dancing lights, and the three-dimensional image beginning to form in front of them seemed even more powerful - more magical - than ever. Mac stole a glance at Nicole as people and things came into focus within the brilliant white globe of light. She smiled at the sight of Nicole's mouth actually hanging completely open.

This vision was different from the others, and not just because it showed a different time or place. It was so bright that the colors were washed out and blurry at the edges of what Mac had come to think of as 'the stage'. She could clearly make out Jared and could tell that he was in a Christmas setting. *We're not too late,* she thought. Other people moved around the edges, coming in and out of focus. As Jared moved, the vision moved with him, keeping him in its center. He had the same loving look on his face that she'd seen before, but she couldn't tell who he was looking at. A woman moved into the vision from behind the group, as if she'd walked through them like a ghost. They could only see her from the back. Mac took in a sharp breath and said, "That's who I saw before. Could it be me?"

As if in answer, another woman appeared from the left side. At first, she was too close to the edge to be identified. Mac was first. "That's me." Mac strode closer to the center of the vision. She was smiling, too, both at Jared and at other people or activities beyond the edges of the light.

"So, who's the one with Jared?" Aaron asked.

"That's the million-dollar question, isn't it?" Mac answered as she shifted her head left and right in a fruitless attempt to see more than the vision was revealing.

"What was that other girl's name?" Nicole asked. "His friend from work."

It hit Mac like a truck. "Andrea. It could be Andrea."

As the vision collapsed around Jared, Mac strained to see details about the woman he was staring at with the dreamy expression Mac thought was for her. The vision was still too bright to make out the exact color of her hair, but it could be the auburn shade Mac recalled. The height and general size were right. But it was a feeling that the mystery woman and Jared were familiar to each other that finally convinced Mac. The way their heads moved in sync when Jared talked. The way his eyes stayed locked on hers when she gestured because he knew what she was saying with her hands. They knew each other better than two people who had just met.

As the song ended, all they could see was the back of Andrea's head and Jared's contented face. Mac wasn't sure she had ever felt as happy as he looked.

Stan broke the silence. "Pretty good use of a quarter, eh?"

Mac answered, "So, what are we going to do about it?"

∼

THE HEADLIGHTS of oncoming cars shone through the windshield and painted the inside of the van with pale light and dancing shadows. Mac watched from the jump seat. No one had spoken since Nicole thanked Mac for letting her ride shotgun. As she said, "No problem," Mac allowed herself to acknowledge that she was - or had been - that kind of person. The kind that sits in the back so a friend can be comfortable. The kind that lets an angry word breeze by because her relationship with the angry speaker was more important than being offended on a bad day. The kind who would help a stranger be happy, even if there was nothing in it for Mac.

"Do you think there's still a chance we can pull this off?" Mac's voice bounced around the back of the van.

Nicole answered, "Why not? I don't think the jukebox would have shown us something that can't come to pass."

"I'm such an idiot." Mac found it easier to be direct while talking to the anonymous vehicles she could see through the back windows.

"Maybe," Aaron said. "But you're less of an idiot now than a week ago. You're enough of a non-idiot to get another chance."

"If only I had caught on sooner. If I had sincerely tried to see what the jukebox was trying to show me instead of what I wanted to see."

"If only you hadn't walked into that diner. If only you weren't a human being with a human need for companionship. If only, if only, if only." Apparently, not having to look at each other made it easier for Aaron to be direct, too.

"Okay, I get it. What can I say? I seem to have a knack for making life harder than it has to be."

"And it can be hard enough on its own, don't you think?" Aaron's voice was kind but distant, as if he was talking to himself as much as to Mac.

"Yes, Aaron, I do think. No more pity parties. It is what it is. I just have to make the best of it from here."

"Did you do that on purpose?" Nicole asked.

"Do what?"

"String a whole Lifetime movie's worth of cliche's together in one sentence."

The laughter carried away the evening's stress and pushed the upcoming worries out of the way for a few minutes. As the road hummed under her at seventy miles an hour, Mac made a promise to herself. No matter what she had to do, Jared was going end up happier than he was when they first met.

CHAPTER 21

Mac had been working on an email to Jared all morning. She had just finished the fifth version but had deleted everything but "Hi, Jared, this is Mac Talley following up on the note I sent the other day." No matter what she wrote, she couldn't picture him replying. She hoped she was wrong but was ready if she was right. After a few more drafts, she clicked the send button and started her mental timer. At the six-hour mark, she sent him a text. "Not trying to bother you, but it's urgent that I speak to you. Please call me."

Nicole, who had been watching Mac struggle, pace, and check her phone a hundred times an hour, came up behind her and put both hands on Mac's shoulders. "Have faith. You'll get through to him one way or another."

"I'm not sure that's true. Honestly, if it were me, I would delete the email and the text without even looking at them. The only thing left to do is to call, but there's no way he answers when he sees my number come up."

"So don't call from your phone. Use the office phone."

"Depending on his caller-id system, he might still know it's me. I could use your phone but, if he's like me, he lets calls go to voice mail if he doesn't recognize the name or number." She continued to stare at her phone as if waiting for it to offer a solution. In a way, it did. She used it to look up the main number for Jared's law firm. Just before launching the call, she told Nicole, "Get out of here unless you want to be an accomplice to fraud and general creepiness."

Nicole didn't move. A man's voice came on the line and Mac almost hung up before realizing that the voice belonged to someone younger and more Texan than Jared. He was still talking when Mac's panic eased from a ten to the expected eight. "Hello? Is anyone there?"

"Yes. Hello. Jared Brownfield, please."

"May I tell him who's calling?"

Mac mouthed the words "Last chance" at Nicole and then said into the phone, "This is Kelly Higgins."

Nicole tilted her head down and regarded Mac sourly over imaginary librarian glasses. Mac mouthed "Warned you" while the Texan intern drawled, "Just a moment, please."

"Hey, Kelly, what's up?"

"Don't hang up. Please."

"Why would I... who is this?"

"It's Mac Talley. Please don't hang up. Give me one minute."

"I should hang up on principle. It's pretty low to impersonate a shared friend. At least I assume you haven't chased her away yet."

"I know. And I wouldn't have done it if I saw any other way."

"One minute. And skip the giant apology. I know you're sorry."

Now off balance, Mac stammered, "Well, that's the whole reason I called. I want to apologize in person. There's a group dinner thing coming up, and I was really hoping you would come. A onetime thing. No ulterior motive. In fact, bring a date."

"Seriously?"

"Seriously."

"Look, Mac, Kelly speaks very highly of you, but I don't know you and, honestly, don't want to. Consider your apology accepted. Move on."

"Is there anything..."

"No. I hope you find a wonderful person who can make you happy, but I don't want to know about it or be any part of it."

Mac expected to hear the tone signaling the end of the call but the line was still open. She marveled at his professional politeness. "I understand. Thank you for listening."

"Goodbye."

Then came the tone.

~

KELLY WAITED until the fifth ring before answering her phone. "Hello?" She knew it was Mac but wanted the extra couple of seconds to finish steeling herself for the conversation. Mac's sweet, sincere email came to mind, making Kelly wonder why talking to her was making her feel so unsettled.

"Hi, Kelly. It's Mac."

"Hey, Mac. Thank you for the kind note. You were way more apologetic than you needed to be. I get it, remember?"

"And I appreciate that. But I realized that I asked a lot from a brand-new friend."

"It's okay." *And now...*, Kelly thought.

"Do you have a minute for me to get you up to speed?" Before Kelly could answer, she continued, "Do you even want to be up to speed?"

"Yes, and yes."

"I wish you could have been there, Kelly. At the diner. The jukebox showed us that it's not too late to help Jared."

"Go on."

"He and I were there but weren't together as a couple. There was a bunch of other people that we couldn't see real well. The place was decorated for Christmas...and I just know it is *this* Christmas. He looked so happy, Kelly."

"What do you think it means?" Kelly had a feeling that whatever Mac thought the vision was telling her was going to need Kelly to do something.

"I think it means we need to put Jared, me, the jukebox, and whoever else we think was in the vision together in one place. According to the counter, there's only one vision left."

"Was I there? Is that why you're calling?"

"I don't think so," Mac said, and then, as what sounded like an afterthought, "but you're welcome to come. You should come."

"Just let me know when and where, and I'll try to be there. Even though I can imagine the visions, it would be nice to see one for myself."

"That's the thing…" Mac said. "… It's going to be tricky to get Jared there. He isn't speaking to me."

Kelly listened as Mac told her about the conversation she'd just had with Jared. Kelly said, "If you're asking me to try and get him to go somewhere or do something, you're probably out of luck. Our last conversation was awkward, to say the least."

"Will you try? I know I have no right to ask you for anything else, but I am really trying to make this right." Kelly felt, more than heard, the desperation in Mac's voice. She said, "I don't know. What, exactly, are we trying to do?"

"The owners of the diner will let us come over any time, but we need to do it between now and Christmas. I'm thinking the 23rd. Christmas Eve is probably out. That's only a few days from now but, hopefully, everybody can make it then or one or two days earlier."

"Just a onetime apology dinner."

"As far as he knows, yes."

Kelly was about to agree to call Jared when Mac added, "Wow. I almost forgot. He needs to bring his friend Andrea with him."

"Why?"

"She was with him in the vision. We think she's the reason he looked so happy."

Kelly's stomach, which had already been sending signals, twisted even more. "Hold on. You think this is all about getting Jared and Andrea together?"

"We do."

"That doesn't sound right. I've seen them together. I can't imagine that relationship going from work friends to romance by Christmas, no matter how much magic is involved." A new thought occurred to Kelly, and she shared it without waiting for Mac to say anything. "Wait. Didn't you say that diner is always decorated for Christmas?"

"Yes. It's sort of their brand."

"So, the jukebox could be showing something that happens weeks or months from now."

"I don't think so. It's the Christmas Jukebox." Mac sounded more certain than Kelly thought she should or could be.

"I'm out, Mac. You're doing a good thing, and I believe the jukebox is channeling some virtuous force to help you. But it seems to me that your Christmas deadline is in your head. If you saw Jared in the diner with the jukebox, Andrea, and a bunch of other people, I think you should take your time. Maybe talk to Andrea and see if you can figure out how far away she is from an office romance. Then schedule your dinner party."

"So you won't call Jared."

"Not now. It doesn't feel right to me. Let's take a break and let Jared's feelings settle. You and Aaron can come up to the ranch after the first of the year and we'll brainstorm."

"That's a sweet offer. Thanks, Kelly."

"No problem. In fact, you can come up for our New Year's Eve party if you want. It's always a blast."

"Thanks. Maybe I will." Mac's tone was low and even. "Gotta go. Talk to you later."

The call ended while Kelly was saying, "Goodbye." She put the phone back in her pocket and resumed wiping down a table in the dining hall. She tried to wipe away the sticky feeling that the universe had plans for her before New Year's.

∽

MAC DOUBTED that Aaron even realized that he was singing softly to himself. He hadn't responded when she walked into the shop and asked what he was up to. Now she could see that he was wiping something on a round side table with impossibly narrow, spindly legs. His back was to her, but she could make out the black bulge of two noise-cancelling earphones connected by a cord. She took a few steps back and called his phone. While continuing to push a cheesecloth rag around with his right hand, he reached up with his left and tapped his ear. "Hello?"

"Turn around," Mac said.

He smiled sheepishly when he saw her. She waved and ended the call. He popped the buds out and let them hang around his neck. A look of panic came to his face as he said, "Hold on a second. I have to keep working this stain or it won't come out even."

Mac watched over his shoulder as he expertly rubbed the table top, turning the rag over in his gloved hand to add a little stain here and remove a little there, until it was a gorgeous reddish brown. Satisfied, he put the rag in an old box and then peeled off the gloves. "That looks really nice," Mac said as she looked at the table from several angles.

"Thanks. Do you recognize it?"

"It's not that pink monstrosity you stripped clean, is it?"

"Sure is. Turns out that whoever desperately wanted a pink table had no idea what they were covering up."

"You'd think that, by now, I wouldn't be surprised when a piece turns out to be a lot different under its finish. But this table is amazing. Who'd have thought?"

Aaron squatted and looked directly across the drying surface. "I was blown away when I scraped off the first bit of paint and saw the actual wood. It was like it's been waiting for me to find it."

"I wasn't even sure it was worth putting in the main gallery. It was headed for the thrift store. Now, it can go front and center. Maybe we put that Tiffany vase on it. I need to update my estimate; should be able to get a couple hundred for it, easy."

"Maybe more." He smiled. "And it's the same table. The only difference is a little time, effort, and a couple dollars' worth of stain and varnish."

"If only I could fix all my problems with a little stain and varnish."

"What do you mean?" Aaron gestured for them to move away from the fumes.

"Jared won't meet with me."

"Not surprised."

"Kelly won't talk to him about it, either."

"Only slightly surprised."

Mac sat down on a short section of reclaimed church pew. Aaron settled in next to her. "I hoped that Kelly would help. She believed in fate before I did. Sure, she hasn't seen a vision, but she believes they're real."

"She's already done a lot. I'm sure she has her reasons not to get involved right now."

"I guess. She did say we could talk again in a few weeks."

"But you think that's too late."

"I don't know how, but I *know* it will be too late. If we don't get Jared and Andrea in the same room with the jukebox before Christmas, this entire stressful month will have been a waste. He'll still be miserable, and it will all be my fault."

"So, what's next?"

"I don't have any idea." She sort of smiled. "I guess I could have the jukebox delivered to his office with a sign that says, 'Play Me'."

"He sounds like a good guy who's been through a lot lately," Aaron said. "Maybe he'll listen to a fellow traveler along the rough road of romance."

"The 'rough road of romance'?"

"How else would you describe it?"

"You'd do that?"

"I'll try. But don't get your hopes up. I doubt I would listen to him if our roles were reversed."

"Thank you, Aaron. You're the best."

"I just scrape paint and add varnish."

CHAPTER 22

Although he had decided not to stop by, Aaron still felt a tug from Starcrest Ranch as he drove past the brick and iron gate. The benefit of hearing Kelly's perspective firsthand wasn't worth the risk of being talked out of his mission. He had a good plan. It felt right and, he thought, had a better-than-even chance of succeeding. Kelly had a way of turning him around, though. It would seem like she was just listening - even agreeing - until the conversation ended and Aaron found himself sharing Kelly's opinion about whatever they'd been discussing. He knew it wasn't deliberate or deceitful on her part. She simply had that kind of personality. He would have to find another base of operations for this trip.

The Starbucks seemed like as good a place as any. He didn't think Jared would recognize him if he bumped into him and, even if he did, Aaron could just jump right in and hope for the best. The morning rush was winding down when Aaron walked in the door and sat at a table against the wall. He used his phone to review the list of restaurants near either the coffee shop or Jared's office. He knew the area pretty well, but restaurants come and go. It wouldn't do to suggest meeting at a place that went out of business a year ago.

At 9:45, he dialed Jared's direct number but didn't touch the send button. His finger was shaking in time with his racing heart. He closed his eyes, reminded himself that it was just a phone call, and touched the button.

"This is Jared."

"Good morning, Jared, this is Aaron Stiles. I'm a friend of Kelly's." The misdirection didn't bother Aaron at all. He was pretty sure he would have to do worse if this was going to turn out the way it needed to.

"Kelly Higgins?"

"That's right."

"What can I do for you?"

Something in the tone of Jared's voice made Aaron abandon the elaborate script he'd prepared. He'd convinced himself that the end justified almost any means as long as the two men ended up in a room together talking about Mac. Now, anything but a straightforward telling of the truth felt wrong. Most of the truth, anyway. Without giving it any more thought, he said, "I think we can do something for each other. Actually, for people we care about."

"What's this about? Is Kelly in trouble?"

"No, she's fine. She's just caught up in the same situation you and I are. And… I'm starting to believe that we are the only ones who can help unravel it all and get people sleeping soundly again."

"I'm listening, but I have no idea what you're talking about."

"When I tell you, you're going to want to hang up on me."

Jared waited a beat, and Aaron could imagine a look of recognition appearing on his face. Jared said, "Maybe I should just hang up now."

"You could, and I wouldn't blame you or bother you again. But I don't think you will."

"Why is that?"

"Because you're a good person who cares about other people. Even other people you don't know very well."

"Like you?"

"Like Mac Talley." Aaron held his breath and stared at his phone, expecting to see 'Call Ended' any second.

When Jared spoke again, Aaron could tell he wasn't surprised to hear Mac's name. "There it is. I should have known."

"But you didn't hang up. That's good. Look, you don't know me. The only things we have in common are two women who met and became friends because of you. I care about them both. Since you're still listening, I'm going to assume that you at least care what happens to Kelly."

"That's true. And I have no hard feelings toward Mac. She just needs to find someone else to obsess over."

"Trust me, she knows. She wants to." Nothing about the conversation up until now had gone according to plan. Aaron jumped right to the end. "I'll tell you what. I'm in town for business. Meet me for lunch and I'll tell you everything you need to know in order to decide whether or not you want to help."

"If we do this and I decide to walk, nobody will mention it to me ever again?"

"Promise. As a bonus, though, you'll know more about what Kelly's been through in case you want to stay friends with her."

"Alright. I only have an hour, so we'll need to meet on the east end of town."

"How about Kenny's?"

"That will be fine. 11:45 at Kenny's."

After he ended the call, Aaron noticed that the staff had turned up the music. He closed his eyes and enjoyed feelings of relief amplified by the tones of "It's Beginning to Look a Lot Like Christmas."

~

KENNY'S WAS NOT the same restaurant Aaron had remembered. White walls, round red tables, and kinetic sculptures took the place of heavy tables, ancient lighting, and hundred-year-old art. Everyone in the place was wearing their uniform. Lawyers wore suits; computer people wore designer tees and jeans with expensive holes in them; women dressed according to the message they wanted to send. There were skirts and blazers, slacks and loose blouses, and the same tee/distressed jeans ensemble that the guys wore.

Aaron was early, hoping to get a table where he could watch the door for Jared. As he talked to the overly-serious host, though, a motion caught his eye. "Never mind," he said, "the guy I'm waiting for is already here."

He was surprised when Jared stood up to greet him. "I'm Jared," he said as he stuck out his hand.

"Aaron. Thanks again for meeting me."

They shook hands and sat down. Jared pushed the menu toward Aaron. "Everything's good here, but the portions are kind of small. If you're hungry, order an appetizer." He picked up his own menu and looked it over. Without looking at Aaron, he said, "I almost stood you up."

"Why didn't you?" Aaron said to his menu.

"Two reasons. First, you didn't try to BS me. At least not that I could tell. Second, I'm curious."

"I'm glad your curiosity got the best of you." Aaron closed his menu and hoped that the new Kenny hadn't changed the barbecue recipe.

"We should get right to it," Jared said after the waitress took their order. "I need to get back as soon as I can."

"Sure. Here's the deal. Mac knows now that what she thought was fate or love at first sight or whatever you want to call it was actually a rebound reflex. She feels terrible about pushing herself on you."

"Rebound reflex?"

"Her boyfriend - a friend of mine too, in fact - just up and left her a couple months ago. No warning, no explanation, and no instructions about running their business. She was in a pretty bad way."

"I'd ask her why she didn't tell me this herself, but I already know the answer. I didn't give her a chance."

"That's right. And the thing is that she's now as obsessed with clearing things up with you as she was with getting together with you."

"Kelly said that Mac was a caring person."

"She is. It tears her up to think you suffered at all because of her. She wants everyone to be happy." Aaron smiled. "And as much as I try to tell her that's not her job, she insists on trying."

"What does she want from me? To accept her apology? That seems too easy."

"It's not much more complicated than that. She has this… vision… that you will hear her out in person, tell her you forgive her, smile sincerely, and walk away happy."

"And if I don't?"

"She'll get over it."

"But…" Jared's voice trailed off as he waited for the rest of Aaron's statement.

"But it will take a while and, in the meantime, those of us who are in her orbit will spend a lot of time patting her on the head. I also can't promise she won't call you in an ice-cream-fueled surge of regret."

"Okay. I'll call her."

Aaron was ready for this response and hoped he could steer the rest of the conversation. "That might work, but I can't guarantee it. The picture in her mind is very clear." He paused for effect. "What I *can* guarantee is that if you accept her invitation to dinner, she will be satisfied and move on, no matter what happens."

Their food arrived and Jared began using his fork to bury croutons. He said, "How is taking her to dinner going to *reduce* her fantasy that we were meant for each other."

"First, that's not her fantasy anymore. Second, we're talking about a group event at a diner in Green Vista. She knows the owners and wants to make a special evening of it. You could bring a date or a friend."

"She mentioned that when she called. I thought it was another ruse."

"No, she is very serious about you not coming alone. She almost insisted on it." Aaron tried to sound as casual as possible when he said, "What about your friend…Adrienne?"

"You mean Andrea?"

"Sorry, that's it. Kelly said you were pretty close."

"We are. She's a talented colleague and a good friend."

Aaron popped a fry in his mouth, captured Jared's eyes in his best deal-closing gaze, and asked, "So what do you say?"

Jared slowly finished chewing. He dabbed at the corners of his mouth with his napkin, and said, "I say I'll think about it."

Aaron ate a victory fry and started on his sandwich. Between bites, he told Jared about the gallery and how he met Mac. Jared explained what kind of law he practiced and how his recent break-up made him react the way he did to Mac's advances.

"I know what you mean," Aaron said. "I was dumped by the love of my life not too long ago."

Jared nodded while he ate and Aaron knew that, if his mouth hadn't been full, Jared would have said, 'I hear you, man' or something like it.

"Actually, you know the girl who ruined me."

"Really? Who?"

"Kelly."

Aaron had no idea why he brought her up, but the look on Jared's face confirmed that he was supposed to mention her. Jared said, "I would have never guessed. You seem to get along okay."

"We do. She's really hard to stay mad at."

"I know what you mean. After I finished helping her with the ranch, I went over the billing, as I always do. Turns out that I did a couple thousand dollars' worth of pro bono work without even realizing it." Jared smiled and looked past Aaron as if Kelly were standing behind him. "She would ask, and I would get the answer or do the favor or whatever. I should have sent her a final bill, but I never got around to it."

It was Aaron's turn to nod.

Jared's smile dimmed to just north of serious, a sparkle in his eyes being the only clue that he was still speaking fondly of his former client. He said, "Trust me. I never let more than a few dollars slide when the client agrees to pay full rates."

They shook hands again. Aaron felt like he was saying goodbye to a friend he ate lunch with regularly. There was something very likable about Jared Brownfield. He would be good for Mac or Andrea, or, probably, almost anyone. No wonder the jukebox was trying to put someone in his life. And vice versa.

CHAPTER 23

"Staring out that window isn't going to make him get here any sooner," Nicole said to a fidgety, pacing Mac.

"I know, I know. I wish he had either told me the whole story or not said anything at all. His 'Good news' text was worse than nothing."

Nicole smiled. "He probably did it on purpose."

"Probably. As long as he really does have good news, I'll let it slide."

By the time Aaron arrived, Mac's determination to play it cool was completely gone. The door hadn't eased shut behind him before she asked, "Well?"

"Well… he'll come to your dinner. He will also bring a date."

"Andrea?"

"Sounded like it. He didn't say for sure, but he definitely has feelings for her. They've been friends for a long time."

"That's great!" She gave Aaron a quick hug, resting her hands on his biceps as she pushed away and asked her next question. "Which day?"

"He couldn't say for sure but seemed open to the week of Christmas. I'm supposed to text him later today to lock in the date."

"Awesome. Isn't this awesome, Nicole?"

"I'm beside myself." Nicole grinned, gently mocking Mac's enthusiasm. With more sincerity in her voice, she added, "I can't wait to meet him."

Mac looked at the group of a dozen clocks on the wall next to the door. Each was set to a different time so she didn't have to constantly keep them in sync. The most expensive one always showed the correct time as a subtle cue to customers that it was the most accurate clock in the store. This week's truth-teller was a hundred-year-old mantle clock. Mac said, "Should you text him now?"

Aaron looked at his phone. "It's only been three hours. Plus, he said he had a busy afternoon ahead. Let's give him some time."

"Come on, Mac," Nicole said as she gestured toward the back of the gallery. "I need you to help me change the pricing on some items that aren't going to move otherwise. I've watched at least six people pick up this snow globe, for instance, and then put it back down like it was full of spiders."

"But that's an antique."

"We can argue about it for up to an hour." Nicole winked at Aaron.

Mac and Nicole were negotiating over a Hummel figurine when Aaron came back just over an hour later. "Who's buying from whom?"

Mac laughed. "It does sound like we're dickering, doesn't it? Once we agree on a price, we update the tag. I think we've stumbled on a pretty good system." Her eyes widened as she emerged from her world of antiques. "Did you text Jared?"

"Yep. That's the good news. The bad news is that he can't make it on the 22nd or the 23rd."

"21st?"

"Nope." Aaron's face was slack, but his eyes were dancing.

"20th?"

"Nope." He let Mac off the hook. "Believe it or not, Christmas Eve works best for him."

"I felt like the vision was showing me Christmas Eve, but I was afraid to hope we could make it happen. Stan and Moira already said they can host us any day, including Christmas. Can you still come help get ready on the 24th?"

"Sure."

"I might not be able to come, Mac," Nicole said quietly.

"Not at all? You said you might be able to stop by but leave early."

"I don't think that will work after all. Mom's sister is coming with her family. I really should be there the whole time." Nicole smiled again and said, "But that's okay. Aaron will be there for moral support, and it's way more important to fit Jared's schedule than mine. I'll get all the details later. You can even call me Christmas morning."

"I will. I absolutely will."

～

MAC SHOVED her phone back into a pocket and wondered when she had become so insecure. Her call to Kelly had gone to voice mail, but that could just mean that she was too busy to answer. Maybe Kelly *was* ignoring her, Mac thought, but worrying about wouldn't do any good. She was already so anxious about the big dinner that Nicole had taken away her coffee and made her drink two glasses of water. But, as long as Jared and the jukebox were in the same room on Christmas Eve, Mac would have fulfilled her obligation to fate. It would be nice, though, she thought, if she could wrap up the whole affair with her friends around. It would match the vision more closely, too.

Right after she set a mental alarm to send Kelly a text just before lunch, her phone rang. It was Kelly. "Hey, Kelly, thanks for calling back so soon."

"No problem. How are you doing? Any progress with Jared?"

"Actually, that's why I called." She rushed ahead before Kelly could worry about being asked to intervene again. "He's agreed to meet for dinner so I can properly apologize, and we can all get closure."

"Wow. I honestly didn't think he would go for that. Good for you. How did you convince him?"

"I didn't. Aaron had a man-to-man with him. And 'meet for dinner' really means show up at the diner for a group Christmas dinner."

"The diner where, coincidentally, the Christmas jukebox stands ready to show him his destiny."

"Coincidentally."

"I hope it works out for him… and you. It has been a wild ride."

"For all of us," Mac added and then asked, "Would you like to come? I could use the moral support and it would mean a lot to me."

"Sure, if I can get away. When is it?"

"That's the thing. Jared can only make it if we meet on Christmas Eve." The line was silent. "I know. It caught me by surprise, too. We suggested the 22nd or 23rd but those nights don't work for him."

"I don't know, Mac. I've got a family reunion booked all week and they expect a special meal on Christmas Eve and Christmas day."

"I understand. No pressure. If you are able to get away, feel free to bring a friend or a date. I'll do it if I have to, but the thought of sitting across from Jared with Stan and Moira being the only other people there makes me queasy."

"So, he's coming alone?"

"I hope not, but you know me. My imagination jumps from worst case to worst case these days."

"I'll see what I can do. Congratulations, by the way. Looks like the jukebox picked the right person after all."

"Nobody could be happier than I will if that turns out to be true when we wake up on Christmas morning. Heaven knows I've taken every possible wrong turn up until now."

"Have faith, my friend."

∼

"You do know that every wreath, garland, and candy cane we put up now will have to come back down in a week or two, right?" Nicole handed the end of a garland up to Mac, who was perched on a step ladder.

"I know, but the place didn't feel quite festive enough."

"It's ten times more festive than last year."

"Richard wasn't interested, and Christmas hasn't been my thing since I was a kid."

"Until this year."

"Until the jukebox." Mac climbed down and admired her handiwork. "I kind of like it. Maybe we'll keep them up all year, like at the diner."

"Another 'Christmas Town' store? I don't think that fits your high end 'antiques and collectibles gallery' branding."

"Listen to Ms. Scrooge," Mac said to Aaron as he walked by, carrying three steaming cups.

"Don't drag me into this," he said with a grin. "I just work here."

"Is that what I think it is?" Mac reached for one of the cups.

"It is if you think it's the best hot chocolate your petty cash fund can buy."

Nicole hopped up to sit on a counter and stuck out her hand. "Just what I need to boost my Christmas spirit."

"To Christmas spirit and Christmas jukeboxes," Mac said as she raised her cup in a Styrofoam toast.

They sipped hot chocolate and enjoyed the comfortable silence until it was interrupted by the sound of the bell announcing a customer.

"Got it," Mac said, as she placed her cup on the desk and headed for the front of the gallery. She stopped a dozen feet away from a middle-aged couple who were admiring the wall of clocks.

"I wonder if that's a real German cuckoo clock," the woman said.

Mac walked closer. "It is. Made by hand in Bavaria during the Second World War. I'm Mac, by the way. Is there something in particular I could help you find?"

"No, dear, we're just browsing," the woman said automatically.

Her companion stepped forward. "Actually, we found your gallery on the Internet and there's something on your site I would like to see in person."

"Certainly," Mac answered, "Assuming we still have it. What are you looking for?"

"It was an old jukebox. A Christmas jukebox, you called it. I've never seen anything like it."

"And he's seen a jukebox or two," the woman, who Mac now assumed was his wife, added.

"I still have it but it's at a different location. It is a unique piece, though, that's for sure."

"What do you know about it? What brand is it?"

"It appears to have been custom made."

"Looks like whoever did it might have started with a Wurlitzer."

"Could be. It does have those beautiful curves," Mac improvised.

"Is it for sale?"

Mac's instinct was to set the hook and start reeling, but it suddenly felt like betraying a friend. "No, I'm afraid not. Not right now, anyway. It's on loan until after the holidays."

"And then?" The man was trying to hide his excitement, but Mac knew he was setting an upper price limit in his head.

"And then… I don't know. I've become rather attached to it."

He smiled. "Are we chatting or negotiating?"

"Chatting." She pulled a business card from a holder on the counter. "You can call me after the first of the year, if you like."

"Do you know how much you would want for it… if you were to sell it? Just ballpark."

"No, Sir. I haven't thought about pricing it since I put the picture online." As the next words came out of her mouth, she knew they were absolutely true and that the man in front of her did not qualify. "If the right buyer came along, I'm sure I would be able to set a fair price."

The couple wandered around for a few more minutes and the wife bought the metal Dr. Pepper sign with what Mac assured them was a real bullet hole. The woman smiled apologetically as Mac rang her up, leaving the impression that she was only buying the sign so everyone could feel good at the end of an awkward encounter. Mac wasn't offended. She had bought the sign under similar pretenses.

As they left, the man waved Mac's business card as he said, "Merry Christmas and Happy New Year. You'll be hearing from me."

Being forced to think about the approaching holiday and the jukebox at the same time started a hum of nervousness in Mac's gut. It would only grow more intense as Christmas Eve approached.

CHAPTER 24

Aaron took the "Merry Christmas! See You Next Week!" sign from the printer tray and slid it into a festive frame. He could fix almost anything but was always pleased when he was able to create something new, no matter how small. It was almost time to leave for the diner and Mac was nowhere to be found. He checked his phone again to make sure his sign-making hadn't distracted him from the buzz of a text. He looked up when the bell on the door rang. A woman was standing just inside, looking down at and adjusting a cream-colored jacket so that it lined up perfectly with her creased matching slacks. Loose curls of auburn hair bounced with every slight movement of her head. Red pumps emerged confidently from beneath creased cuffs. As Aaron's eyes moved back up to the woman's face, they paused as her raised head revealed a red scarf sprinkled with green holly leaves.

"I'm never doing *that* again," she said. Aaron felt himself blush as he took in sculpted cheek bones, long lashes over smokey eyes, and lips as red as the scarf and shoes. Mac was stunning.

"Do what?" he half-stammered.

"Turn myself over to an over-zealous beautician."

"I think they call themselves 'stylists' now."

"Whatever. *This*," she said as she turned in a circle, "is not what I was expecting. I didn't think I was ever going to get out of there."

"You look really nice." Aaron hoped she hadn't seen him check her out when he thought she was a customer.

"Thanks. Is it too much? To be fair, the outfit is my fault. Well, Nicole helped me pick it out, but I put it on, right?"

"Right."

"So is it?"

"Is it what?"

"Is it too much?"

"You are hosting an exclusive Christmas Eve soiree."

"At a diner."

"True. It might be a *little* too much."

"Ugh. I knew we forgot something. Dress code." Mac's eyes pled with Aaron to say something comforting. No amount of expensive makeup could hide the vulnerable yet determined woman he had come to know so well.

"Look, Mac, don't worry about it. I was just teasing… and taking advantage of a rare opportunity to use the word 'soiree' in a real conversation. It's a holiday dinner with friends at a diner. I don't think you need to dress for what might or might not happen. Just be Mac."

She nodded. "I need to change." She looked at the special clock. "But I don't think I have time."

"Tell you what. I know we agreed to take separate cars in case you get caught up in whatever happens with the jukebox, but let's just go together. I'll drop you off to change clothes and then swing by the store to pick up the sodas you promised to bring. We should still get there in plenty of time."

"That would be great. Thanks."

"We can even take my car instead of the van." He turned off the main lights, leaving the store aglow with too many strings of Christmas lights.

"Outside," Aaron texted Mac as he idled in front of her apartment building. A mixed Mac appeared a minute later. She had replaced the jacket and slacks with a silky blouse half tucked into her best jeans, which were tucked into cowboy boots. The scarf hung easily around her neck, as if she was allowing it to come along. Her hair wasn't as carefully coiffed as before but, somehow, more perfect. Most of the makeup was gone, but she was freshening the Rudolph red lipstick as she walked to the car.

"I had to keep the lipstick." She tugged at the scarf. "Matches the scarf."

"Good choice. *Now* you look like you're ready to host the hillbilly holiday hoedown."

She punched him in the arm. "Thanks for trying to keep me sane. I hope you succeed."

He responded by smiling and pulling away from the curb and into traffic. They rode in silence while Aaron jostled with the scores of other drivers escaping the Dallas area for the holiday weekend. Every few minutes, he would sneak a glimpse at Mac. She stared straight out the windshield, obviously remembering or anticipating something big.

They were alone on a stretch of state highway when, without looking his way, Mac spoke. "Can I tell you something?"

He squeezed the steering wheel. "Sure."

"The makeover this afternoon wasn't an accident." After waiting for a response he wasn't ready to give, Mac continued, "I wanted Jared to see the best, most beautiful me." She turned her head and considered Aaron. "You see, the more I thought over all the visions, the more I wondered if maybe I read them right the first time. What if all the drama leading up to tonight was really meant to open his mind and change my approach?"

"Fickle fate."

"Exactly!" She scowled and reconsidered. "I guess. Why was it wrong to assume I knew what the jukebox was telling me at first but now It's okay to put him together with someone I don't even know? Why was I even in the visions to start with?"

"Good questions. I don't know what to tell you, Mac." He looked at her and away from the road for as long as he dared. "So why did you change clothes and ditch the makeup?"

"You made me feel silly," she said without a hint of accusation.

"I didn't mean to."

"Oh, no, you didn't do anything wrong. Seeing you see me made me feel silly. Does that even make any sense?"

"I guess so. Maybe I was a preview of what you thought Jared would see or how he would react."

"I don't know. It felt right when I was sitting under a blow drier, but then felt just as wrong when I walked into the gallery."

"Do you want my advice?"

"Please."

"Quit trying to outsmart an enchanted jukebox. If you really believe it is acting on behalf of fate or the universe, or some other benevolent force, just let it do its job tonight. I've watched you go from confused skeptic to obsessive…"

"… stalker," Mac interjected.

"… stalker to the selfless friend of someone who doesn't want one. Whatever happens, happens. Maybe you took a wrong turn in the beginning, but you've more than made up for it. Sit back and watch the jukebox do its thing… or not. Either way, there isn't anything more you can do."

"You're a good guy, Aaron Stiles. Makes me wonder how Kelly let you get away."

"Fate, I guess."

∽

THE PARKING LOT was empty when Aaron pulled up to the diner, but the white, green, and red lights of Christmas spilled out of the big windows and into the dusk. "Ready?" Aaron asked as Mac watched Stan and Moira scurry around the diner.

"As ready as I'll ever be."

Aaron held the door open for Mac, providing an unobstructed path into Moira's embrace. "Hello, dear, isn't this exciting?"

"Exciting and a little scary. Thanks again for doing all this." Mac stepped back and tried to make a gesture big enough to take in the whole room.

"We're happy to help, aren't we Stan?"

"What can we do to help get ready for dinner? The others should be here in half an hour or so."

"Actually…" Stan said, "We were so excited about your project and Christmas and the jukebox that we got an early start. Everything's ready to go. I just need to drop the fries and grill whatever you all want to eat."

"I even made one of my world-famous carrot cakes," Moira added. "Best you've ever had, guaranteed." She blushed. "If I do say so myself."

Mac's grimaced at the thought of spending thirty minutes doing nothing but anticipating Jared's arrival. Aaron jumped into the silence by saying, "I can hardly wait to try your cake, Ms. Caldwell."

"Moira, please. I know I'm old enough to be Ms. Caldwell, but I like to hear my first name. Especially from my friends."

While Aaron and Moira talked, Mac took the few steps over to the jukebox. It glowed and hummed quietly. She put her hand on the peak of its curved top. Rather than the cool slickness she expected from the polished varnish, the machine was warm. It almost seemed to rise to meet her palm like a loyal dog anticipating its master's touch.

Stan came up behind her. "Are you two ready for the big event?"

"I think I am, but I can't speak for Aaron."

"I wasn't talking about Aaron. I meant your magical partner here." He patted the jukebox, his hand brushing Mac's.

"I just hope I'm not too late. I missed so many signs and who knows how many opportunities."

"Don't worry about it." He stepped forward and waited for Mac to look at him. "Let me ask you a question. What's the best thing that can happen tonight?"

An image of her and Jared walking out of the diner hand in hand came into her mind. As she imagined what it would feel like, the jukebox seemed to cool and retreat from beneath her hand. The last vision replayed in her memory. She answered Stan honestly and with conviction. "The best thing that can happen is for Jared to leave here happy and on whatever path the jukebox meant to put him on."

Stan nodded his approval. "Then don't worry about it." He patted the jukebox again. "Let it do its thing."

Mac smiled and gave the machine a final pat of her own before turning back toward Aaron and Moira. They were chatting quietly, and Mac heard Aaron say her name. Moira laughed with one hand covering her mouth as she snuck a guilty glance at Mac.

"Do I even want to know what you're saying about me?" Mac asked Aaron.

"I was just telling Moira about your remarkable sense of hearing."

Moira laughed again and turned to Mac. "He is a charming young man, you know."

"Don't encourage him," Mac said with a smile that, for the moment, chased away her anxiety.

"I don't need any encouragement. My charm is on autopilot."

"Okay, Aaron," Stan said as he guided Moira into one side of a booth and slid in next to her. "Aim your charm somewhere else. This gal is taken."

Aaron and Mac filled the other half of the booth. Aaron said, "Tell me the story of the jukebox and the Caldwells."

Mac half listened to Stan repeat what he told her when she brought the jukebox home. She had unwittingly sat on the wrong side of the booth. A clock hung on the wall directly in her line of sight. The minute hand squeezed the space between it and the simple black six. Mac's stomach squeezed along with it.

CHAPTER 25

At precisely six-thirty, a pair of headlights signaled the arrival of the next guest. Mac performed a mental fist pump when she caught a quick glimpse of Andrea's auburn hair through the front window. Mac's brain was still formulating a greeting when her eyes settled on a different, but familiar, face. "Kelly?"

"Yep, It's me. Sorry I didn't call ahead; I didn't know until this afternoon that I was going to be able to come. Kimi convinced me that she's ready to be in charge of more than soup and salad."

Mac rushed to her and wrapped her in an embrace. "Thanks for coming. Merry Christmas."

"Merry Christmas to you, too."

As Mac stepped back, she pointed at Kelly's hair. "I love the hair. Almost didn't recognize you. Don't get me wrong, though, I loved the flaming red, too."

"Believe it or not, this is my natural color."

"And I thought you were just trying to copy me." Mac reached up and bounced one of her own fresh curls.

"Nope, I paid good money to get back what God gave me."

"Well, you look great," Aaron said as he took his turn hugging Kelly. "It's great to see you."

"You, too."

Mac noticed that headlights still glowed outside. "Are you alone?"

"No," Kelly answered with a smile. "I came with a friend. He's making a call but should be right in."

Before Mac could ask the obvious next question, Stan stepped between her and Kelly. "I'm Stan. I run this place." He pulled Moira in close. "Actually, she runs both me and this place but lets me pretend."

"Hi, I'm Moira."

"You're the jukebox couple."

"That's right." Stan cocked his head. "Are you acquainted with the Christmas jukebox?"

"Indirectly. I know it's caused all sorts of excitement for Mac."

"And everyone around me," Mac interjected. "If it weren't for Kelly, we wouldn't be here at all." She gave a surprised Kelly another hug. "I'm so glad you could come."

"Me, too. I hope the night goes the way you want it to."

"You mean the way *the universe* wants it to." Mac grinned and Kelly nodded.

The easy balance of new and old friendship shifted when the diner's door opened. Jared came in, but only far enough for the door to close without hitting him. It seemed like everyone was waiting for Mac to break the silence, but she had no words.

Aaron finally stepped forward and extended his hand. "Merry Christmas, Jared. We're glad you made it." He didn't wait for Jared to reply. "Let's see... you know Kelly and Mac... sort of." He shot Jared a hopeful grin. "These fine folks are Stan and Moira. This is their diner."

"For now, anyway," Stan said. "We're *trying* to retire."

"Nice to meet you," Jared said.

Aaron then asked the question that was trapped in Mac's throat. "Did you bring Andrea?"

Jared glanced at Kelly and answered, "I tried to. Something came up this morning and she had to bow out. I'm embarrassed to admit it, but I almost cancelled, too. I just couldn't see myself coming here alone."

"I get it, trust me," Aaron said.

THE CHRISTMAS JUKEBOX

"Luckily, I thought to call Kelly. It took a little convincing but, well, here we are."

Kelly turned so that only Mac could see her face. Then she mouthed, "You're welcome."

Mac found her voice. "So, Jared was the friend on the phone. Smooth move, Kelly." Everyone else in the room was between Mac and Jared when she said, "Thank you for coming. Merry Christmas."

"Merry Christmas," Jared answered.

"I hope you weren't expecting a traditional Christmas meal," Moira said as she licked the end of a pencil. "It's not turkey or goose, but it will be the best diner food you've ever had." She started with Aaron. "Chicken or burger?"

"Burger, of course."

"And to drink?"

"This is Texas, right? Dr. Pepper!"

"What about you... Jared, isn't it? What can I get you?"

Jared poked a thumb toward Aaron. "Same as Aaron."

After writing down Jared's order, Moira said, "Oh, my, look at us all standing around. Please, sit," she said with a wave toward two tables pushed together in the middle of the room. In their unconscious drive to be as far apart as possible, Mac and Jared ended up staring at each other from opposite ends of the tables.

∼

JARED TRIED NOT to watch Mac eat but, every time he looked up, there she was. He could tell from the way her eyes moved from left to right, deliberately jumping past his, that she was having the same problem. He dipped a fry in Stan's "special sauce" letting it hang over the plate while he answered Moira's question about what he did for a living.

As he chewed the French fry, he glanced again at Mac. She met his eyes, smiled almost sheepishly, and touched the corner of her mouth. He did the same and his fingertip came away orange. He nodded his thanks, but Mac had already turned to chat with Kelly.

"Is that how you met Mac? As a client?" Moira asked. Her plate was untouched. Eating was evidently a secondary priority.

"Sort of," Jared answered, trying to be diplomatic. "Kelly introduced us. I did work for her a couple years ago."

"Well, that explains why you and Kelly rode together. Did you become close while working together?"

Jared was forming another semi-answer when Stan rescued him by saying, "Only burgers and chicken breasts are supposed to get grilled tonight, dear. Let the man finish those fries before the warranty expires."

"Sorry, Jared, old habits."

"No problem. The food is great, by the way."

"Wait until you taste the carrot cake. You won't need any other Christmas presents this year," Stan said.

"Don't over-sell it, Honey. Not everyone loves it as much as you do."

"That's their problem."

Movement at the other end of the table caught Jared's eye. Mac was fidgeting. She wiped her hands on her pants as she stood up. He couldn't look away as she walked tentatively to the jukebox and, with a serious look on her face, put a quarter into the slot. As the carousel started to move inside the machine, she looked nervously around the room, deliberately avoiding Jared. A record fell into place and "Jingle Bell Rock" began to play. Mac stared into the jukebox for a few seconds and then returned to her seat. She looked disappointed, as if the machine had played the wrong song.

Stan must have noticed her discomfort because he stood up and announced, "Time for cake, everyone. But first, who needs a doggy bag?"

Jared looked down at his half-eaten fries but decided not to take them home. Aaron, on the other hand, raised a hand and said, "I could have sworn I had some fries left but can't seem to locate them."

Stan mirrored Aaron's sly grin. "Don't worry. Happens all the time. I'll replace them with a fresh batch on your way out."

A small plate holding a big piece of cake appeared in Jared's peripheral vision. "Are you glad you came?" Mac folded her arms across her chest after putting the plate in front of him.

"Yes. It's been nice. You're all very nice."

She hesitated before saying, "I'm glad you came." He believed her.

Mac walked back to the jukebox and put in another quarter. Again, it seemed like more of a ritual than a transaction. Again, she reacted to "What Child Is This?" as if the jukebox had failed to deliver exactly what she paid for.

He watched her as they ate Moira's signature carrot cake. It was delicious, and he told the beaming Caldwells that it was, indeed, the best he'd ever had. He would have to have it again sometime when he wasn't so uncomfortable. Mac's behavior had changed. She ate slowly and asked Kelly to repeat herself twice as they chatted. The sweet, hopeful, but tentative woman who greeted him was gone, replaced by someone who appeared to be ready to fall apart. He couldn't be there when it happened.

∽

Mac's already frazzled nerves found enough energy for one more jolt as Jared walked over and leaned in close. "I'm sorry, but I need to get going. It's a long drive and I don't do well when I get tired."

"I know what you mean. I'm the same way." She stood, not knowing what she was going to say next but being sure that she had to do something before letting him go. She addressed the group. "Hey, guys, Jared needs to leave. Kelly, we can drop you at the ranch if you aren't ready to leave yet."

"That would be great," she answered, taking Mac's subtle cue.

"Stan and Moira, thank you so much for the wonderful food. This is a great diner. I hate to see it close."

"You're welcome and, sometimes, I hate to think of it staying empty, too," Stan answered.

"If you hold on one more minute, I'll box up a piece of cake for the road," Moira added. It wasn't a question.

"Thank you." He turned to Kelly. "I really appreciate you coming with me tonight." Kelly just nodded. To Aaron, Jared said, "Mac's lucky to have a friend like you. I'm still not sure how you turned me around, but I'm happy you did."

"No problem. Glad it worked out."

"Merry Christmas, everyone," Jared said as he walked toward the door.

Mac followed him and, for the first time all night, stood close enough to smell his cologne. "Hold on a second, please." She looked down for a beat and then met his eyes, determined not to look away until she was finished. "First of all, thank you for doing this. For giving me a chance to prove that I'm not a crazy stalker. I hope I did that."

"You did."

"Also, I want to apologize. I had a whole speech ready that tried to explain what I felt for you and why I felt it. But that wouldn't be an apology. That would be therapy."

"It's okay. Really."

"No, it's not okay. When I first saw you, I imagined what we'd be like together, but it was all about me. It took me too long to realize that it's about you. It's always about the other person. Should be, anyway. I'm sorry you had to suffer so I could learn but, on the other hand, I'm glad it was you. You're a good person."

"Not *that* good. I said some pretty mean things to you."

"I deserved everything you said and more. Plus, you didn't have to come tonight."

"I'm glad I did."

Mac held out her hand. "Merry Christmas, Jared Brownfield. And Happy New Year."

"Merry Christmas to you, too." He shook her hand but released it quickly.

As he reached for the door, he hesitated and then walked the few steps over to the jukebox. "This is nice."

Her heart in her throat, all Mac could say was, "Mmm Hmm."

He looked past Mac at Stan and Moira. "My dad collected these things. When I came in, I thought this was just an old Wurlitzer but it's not, is it?"

Stan winked at Mac. "You'll have to ask its owner."

Mac knew what was going to happen next just as surely as if the jukebox had shown her. She handed Jared her last quarter. "Give it a try."

The quarter hit the bottom of the coin box. Jared bent down so he could watch Santa's sleigh begin its short mechanical trip. The carousel turned in almost a full circle until the arm plucked a record from its slot. It settled into place and the lead in to "Have Yourself a Merry Little Christmas" came through the machine's two speakers. Someone turned off the overhead lights, leaving the diner bathed in the glow of Christmas bulbs and the lights from the jukebox dancing across the ceiling. Mac said a prayer of thanks as the lights grew more intense along with the music.

Jared stepped back as the miniature vignette he'd been staring at through the jukebox's window burst out in a blaze of white light. Everyone else instinctively moved away from the center of the diner as the vision took over the space above the tables. During a quiet moment early in the song, Mac heard Kelly whisper, "Oh, my."

The vision showed a broader, clearer version of one it had displayed before. It was set in the diner, but the place was decorated slightly differently than it was now. The image of Jared came into focus first. He was sitting in a booth looking lovingly across the table at a woman who was rummaging through her purse. Her auburn hair obscured her face. Aaron came into view next, as if emerging from the darkness into the center of a brilliant spotlight. He stopped, smiled contentedly, and looked at someone or something that was still out of sight across from him. He reached out as another pair of arms pierced the shaft of light, taking both his hands in hers. The woman with the purse looked over just as the sphere of light expanded to reveal Mac holding Aaron's hands.

In the vision, Jared stood and took his companion by the hand. A toss of her head shook the hair away from her face. From Kelly's face.

As she got out of the booth, she pulled Jared's hand around her waist and planted a kiss on his cheek. He pulled her close and they began to dance. Aaron and Mac danced, too.

As the music ended and the vision dissolved, Mac was the only one who noticed the counter clicking down to zero.

CHAPTER 26

As she balanced with a foot on the booth's bench and a knee on the table, Mac puzzled over the paradox. Was she hanging the wreath because she saw it in the vision, or was it in the vision because she hung it there? "Too bad you've quit talking," she said to the jukebox.

"What's that?" Aaron said from behind the counter.

"Nothing. I was just talking to the jukebox."

"Umm. Okay. It's been silent for a year, so I doubt you're going to get an answer."

"That's what I said."

Aaron lifted the section of counter that separated cook from customer and walked over to Mac. He put his hands on her waist and said, "The kitchen is all set. What else can I do to help get ready for tonight?"

Mac took a step forward and rested her head on Aaron's chest. "Not a thing. That is unless you can make the last few jitters go away. I shouldn't be nervous, but I am."

"They're all friends now, Mac. It's going to be fine. You're going to be fine. Just enjoy it."

Nicole and Richard were the first to arrive. Richard shook Aaron's hand while Nicole and Mac embraced. Mac said, "How's the gallery doing?" She tossed her head toward Richard without looking at him. "You keeping your partner in line?"

"Pretty much." She took Richard's hand in hers. "For some reason, he's still a little gun-shy."

"That's 'cause he knows what will happen if he does you wrong." Mac punched Richard in the arm.

"Don't worry," he said, "I learned my lesson. Leaving you… leaving you all was the stupidest thing I ever did."

"It turned out okay," Nicole said while looking at Mac and Aaron.

"Really," Aaron said. "How's the gallery doing? The website looks good. Are you selling much online?"

"Tons, thanks to Nicole," Richard answered. "She has a gift for it."

"I was struggling a bit, to be honest," Nicole said. "The web sales part came naturally, but I never was good at recognizing the right buys." She turned to Mac. "That was your department. I still haven't met anyone better at it."

"Hey, there, who do you think taught her?" Richard said with a chuckle.

"Sounds like you two make a good team," Mac said, while giving them each a sincere smile. It had taken her the better part of a year and an amateur therapist named Aaron to get to this point.

"What about you guys?" Nicole asked.

"We're doing great," Aaron answered. "Stan and Moira gave us a great deal on this place. Now, I make the burgers and Mac sells the junk."

"It's not 'junk'. We sell antiques and collectibles, just like before. We just do it out of a storage building instead of a gallery," Mac corrected.

"We'll be competing with you online before much longer," Aaron said.

"But don't worry," Mac interjected, "We plan to focus on Christmas collectibles."

When Jared and Kelly came in, the handshake and hug routine repeated. Once everyone was caught up on how the ranch and law practice were going, Aaron went to the kitchen to grill the burgers.

Kelly and Jared joined Nicole and Richard in a booth and the two couples started to get acquainted. Mac watched Jared watch Kelly.

Jared got out of the booth and went over to the jukebox. "This thing still work?"

"Just in the normal way. You were here for the last special event," Mac answered.

He put in a quarter. The carousel turned almost all the way around before dropping a record on the platter. Mac and Jared exchanged a nervous look as "Baby, It's Cold Outside" began to play. Then Jared took Kelly by the hand and they began to dance. Nicole and Richard joined in.

Halfway through the song, Aaron came up behind Mac and asked, "Wanna dance?" She turned and took his hands in hers. They stood like that for a few seconds, just swaying and looking into each other's eyes. Aaron drew Mac in close and they rocked back and forth in time to the music.

When the music stopped, six people remained in three embraces. Six souls were completely content. Seven, counting the Christmas jukebox.

EPILOGUE

"Do you see what I see?" Aaron asked Mac under his breath.

Mac was busy organizing a display case in the newly-opened 'Christmas Town' addition to the diner. She answered, "Apparently not. What am I looking for?"

Aaron pointed to a customer he'd just finished serving. The man appeared to be in his mid-twenties and was all cowboy. He had already paid his tab, added ten gallons to his already towering height, and was headed for the door. The hair on Mac's arms stood on end as he took his hat back off and studied the jukebox.

"That's the third time he's checked it out," Aaron said. "Should we say something?"

She put an arm around his waist. "I don't think so. If I learned anything from our adventure together, it was that the jukebox knows what it's doing."

Aaron replied, "Do you think this guy's the one?"

As if to answer her question, the cowboy came over to them with his hat in his hands. He said, "That jukebox over there. I haven't seen one like it anywhere."

"It came with the diner," Mac fibbed. "We bought the place a couple years ago and thought the jukebox was a great fit for our Christmas theme."

"I'm a collector," the cowboy began, "and I just started picking up pinball machines and video games. I don't have any jukeboxes yet."

"You have a lot to choose from if you want to stick with the '50s and '80s to match your games." Mac decided to test the man's resolve. She remembered the way the jukebox tugged at her the first time she saw it. She added, "A custom piece like this is just as likely to be a waste of money as it is to be a good investment."

"Not that it's even for sale," Aaron added. "If that's what you're driving at."

"Honestly, I don't know *what* I'm driving at. I haven't even considered buying a jukebox. Haven't done any research or anything. My accountant would birth a steer if she were here right now."

"What about your wife?" Mac asked.

"Well, Ma'am, that's a long story with a short ending. Not married."

"Your accountant would probably feel okay if you bought a Wurlitzer in good shape from a reputable dealer. They're not cheap, but they will appreciate."

"No chance you'd part with yours?"

"You don't even know if it works," Aaron said as he offered a quarter.

The cowboy walked over, put the quarter partway into the slot, and then turned around. "How do I pick the song?"

"You don't," Mac answered. "The jukebox plays what it wants you to hear."

While the machine played "Silent Night," Mac and Aaron joined the cowboy as he watched the sleigh fly and the lights dance. When the song ended, the counter clicked and whirred from zero to twelve. "What does that mean?"

"It means we might be able to make a deal."

ABOUT THE AUTHORS

Jason F. Wright is the New York Times bestselling author of Christmas Jars, The Wednesday Letters, and a dozen other books. His latest is an inspiring nonfiction project called See, Love, Lift: How Seeing, Loving, and Lifting Others Will Change Your Life. Like all his titles, it is available on Amazon or from his website at www.jasonfwright.com

John S. Wright is a consultant and technical writer by day and an aspiring storyteller by night.

Made in the USA
Columbia, SC
13 November 2024